THE CHEETAH MYSTERY

HAN PEETERS

FACTION

1

First edition: October 2018
©Han Peeters

ISBN Paperback: 978-94-6217-106-0
ISBN Ebook: 978-94-6217-107-7
NUR: 340

Publisher:
ClusterEffect, Prinsenbeek, The Netherlands
www.clustereffect.nl

With special thanks to:
Ina de Zwart, Frankie Sutton and Aad Vlag

Chapter 1

That morning, Lex Arenberg - Lotharingen cursed under his breath while he read his newspaper. Large headlines told him that the black widow, as she was called in his circles, had earned forty million euros. This had to do with the IPO of a company of which she owned many shares, thanks to her family. He vividly remembered how the 'slut of the underworld', as she was also called, had introduced herself to that family and had exerted her bad influence on her future husband in order to control him. At the time, Lex and his brotherhood had been able to prevent her from attracting too much influence, but her excesses were of such a nature that they had no limits, and for this, she and her husband and co-founder would one day pay a high price. Still worse, this would have a negative impact on all noble families and brotherhoods in Europe with widespread branches all over the world. Eventually, the situation became intolerable and that is why she was now called 'the black widow'. Lex was not so much bothered by her extravagant antics, but rather by the fact that she had managed to amass such a fortune. He would also like to cash in enormously with a simple deal, but this was not an option for him. The old family capital was tied up. In addition, according to his grandfather's will, no one could ever change that. Lex depended on the small dividend - together still a few tons a year - that he obtained from his shares in companies. These were exclusively zoos, dolphinariums and other locations where wild animals were kept captive for education and entertainment. In the 1950s, all blue blood families gained the insight that the common people no longer accepted that the nobility hunted the big five in Africa and they exchanged the guns for photo and film cameras. His grandfather had followed the line that had been set out by the Bilderberg Group and had invested all his money in such low-profit companies, where it would stay forever. Lex hated it intensely. When someone knocked on the door, he was startled.

   'Come in,' he called.

Like every morning around this time, Elena, the maid, stepped into his office with a silver tray in her hands on which his mail was stacked in order of importance, as far as this was visible from the outside of the envelope. The Romanian girl was dressed in a frivolous style, which Lex liked very much. She was wearing a short black skirt with a white apron in front and a black top with short sleeves and a square deeply cut décolleté, trimmed with white piping. Her white long stockings adorned her beautiful long legs and her black pumps completed the voluptuous picture for Lex. The young and attractive woman smiled faintly at him. As was expected of her, she walked around his broad antique desk and stood to his right, where she placed the tray on the table, but held on to it. In that slightly bent position, she felt his hand slip under her skirt and panties as Lex touched her up, just as he did every day. She contracted her buttocks

4

slightly, which excited him, but not so much that he took further action. Lex rubbed her buttocks extensively and squeezed them. Many women would have cried blue murder, threatened with a lawsuit, and started a MeToo discussion about him, but she did not do any of these things. She was cleverer than that. In comparison to what she had to endure since childhood, this was of a very innocent level for her. He had her in his power and this was just part of it.

She did not find Lex unattractive for a man of some sixty years of age. Nobody knew his age exactly because he never celebrated his birthday. Despite the morning ritual, she thought he was a charming man with a resemblance to an older Gregory Peck. In addition, he was a very disturbed person and there were stories about his compulsive personality disorders, and their secret was only one of those. It had been going on for two years, and he had never urged her to do more than what he did to her every morning.

In the blink of an eye, she had been taken from Romania and ended up in this castle, which was located south of Antwerp as she found out later. She had woken up in one of the attic rooms and could not remember anything from the previous day. She had no idea who had kidnapped her nor how she had been transported. However, her body was covered in bruises and she had pain in her bum. When she later told this story, it led to much hilarity among the other staff, whom she considered her close and sweet family. Lex had confiscated her passport and she received no salary for her household services. Furthermore, she was not allowed to contact anyone from outside, but this was not much of a problem for her. The world had been very bad for her and she wanted to hide away the pain she felt when she thought of her past. She was well taken care of now, had good food and she enjoyed the relationships with her new family members. Despite the lack of a salary, she received some money thanks to her cleverness, such as from the gardener's son. Lex regularly sent him out to buy cocaine with cash and then there was always something in it for her, because the cocaine was blended and the son could keep a little business for other users outside the castle. She had once asked him how he blended the cocaine and he had given her the disconcerting answer 'asbestos', after which he laughed loudly, and corrected it to baking powder. She had no expenses, so she saved her money for a time when she might need it. For the time being, she had no desire to flee.

'Your visitor has just arrived,' she said when Lex had stopped his business with her.

'Let him wait in the hunting room,' Lex said, 'and make sure a pot of coffee is ready when I arrive in about fifteen minutes.'

She nodded and bent her knees slightly. Like an experienced model, she held herself completely straight as she walked out of the room and knew that his piercing eyes were pinned to her buttocks. She went down to the basement taking the stairs for the staff that were in the room next to the large wooden staircase in the hall. There she passed the order for coffee to Dione, the butler's wife. In this castle, the butler was always referred to as the Camerlengo, because 'butler' sounded too ordinary. It was a title reserved for church leaders, but Lex did not care about that. According to him, Camerlengo was a better name, which meant that it was not just a butler, but also his personal assistant. In addition, the title had existed in the family since time immemorial. Elena got on very well with Dione and her husband, Charles.

'I'll take care of the coffee,' Dione said, 'because with your little outfit, the visitor will think he ended up in a brothel.'

They both laughed, and in passing, Dione could not resist patting her behind. Elena pretended to have been given a firm blow of the hammer and continued in a feigned crippled walk into the black and white tiled corridor. So she walked to her room to change clothes for the other activities that were planned for her for the day. Dione was still standing at the beginning of the long corridor where she burst out laughing.

Chapter 2

'Welcome,' Lex said when he had entered the hunting
room, 'and I'm sorry you had to wait.'
The men shook hands.

'No problem,' Hector Almagnac - le Noir replied. 'In the
meantime, I have been able to enjoy the collection on
your walls. The last time I was here those trophies were, I
believe, in the hall and on the stairway.'

'That's right,' Lex said, 'for a few years now, we have
rented the chapel of the castle and also the adjoining
room for weddings. Some couples and guests were
disturbed by the stuffed animals and antlers. That's why
we removed them and have set up a special room for
them.'

Lex pointed out a pair of antlers and he briefly told where
and by whom the animal in question had been shot. He
did the same for the prominent polar bear that stood in
the corner and had been holding his claws up for a
hundred years. The animal towered more than a meter
above Lex's slender body. Hector, who estimated himself
to be ten years younger than his host, was stocky. In
recent years, he had insufficiently looked after his health
and he regarded his stocky body as 'a bit above the target
weight', but in reality, it came down to being overweight.
Hector was bald and had a slightly drooping double chin.
He envied his host for whom the years had been mild. In
contrast to Lex, Hector did not have such a vibrant
appearance.

'One thing has kept me busy, especially while I was waiting for you, and that was this picture,' Hector said, and walked towards the wall.

The photo was slightly above the fine wood paneling at eye level.

'What I see is that a large animal has been shot and the hunters are proud of what they did. It is a black-and-white photograph, which made me think it was a scene from about a hundred years ago, but when I took a closer look, I saw that the animal is probably a triceratops, as can be seen from his two horns, the horn on his nose and the bone collar in his neck. I think that's very quaint. '

It provoked a hearty laugh from the host.

'The indignation was overwhelming when this picture was published,' Lex said, 'and the three men you see here with their broad smiles and folded guns faced death threats. Of course, it is impossible, because the animal has been extinct for some 65 million years. The photo was meant as a joke and was made on the film set of Jurassic Park. Therefore, you see how easy it is to influence people through a photo. Many find it difficult to make a clear distinction between fact and fiction, which often plays tricks on their limited intellectual faculties. This photo became a great promotion for the film. It hardly cost a thing and the media fell over each other with laughter at the suckers who thought that a massacre had taken place. Funnily enough, this is the reason for which I have invited you, but I will come to that later. First, I would like to know how you are doing.' Lex invited his guest to sit down in a leather chesterfield armchair and he placed himself opposite him in an identical chair. A bell and a tray with a silver coffee service had been placed on the round coffee table between them. Lex picked up the bell with his thumb and forefinger and let it ring, which was the sign for Dione to open the door of the hunting room.

'Dione, could you please pour us a cup of coffee. Then you can go and we will look after ourselves.'
With a steady hand, Dione picked up the coffee pot from the hot plate that was heated with a tea light and she performed her task with great dedication, after which she left the room.

'So, my dear Hector, tell me, how are you doing? And I also want to know everything about your son, who has ambitious plans, as I have understood from a number of members of our fraternity.'
Hector had only been a member of the order for twenty years and had lived abroad for the past few years. Within the ranks of the order, he had not climbed further than the status of apprentice and the last time they talked extensively, was about ten years ago when Hector had done a job for Lex.

'As you know, we returned from South Africa a few months ago. It is a beautiful country, but it is no longer safe for white people. Certainly not for those who live remote. My wife was startled when she saw through the curtains of our bedroom that a bushman with a gun was standing on the porch. You understand that it was for me, the proverbial straw as well. We actually had enough of it, and now we live near Reims where we can live freely and are better protected to our complete satisfaction, but how is your wife, if I may ask?'

Lex understood that his guest did not want to divulge much more and therefore asked him a counter-question.

'Reims,' Lex said, 'that's just over an hour away from the fraternity by car. Can I assume that you will again visit our order frequently and take part in the events?' Hector confirmed by nodding his head and Lex continued,

'My wife, Amélie, is doing very well. She is enthusiastically organizing the renting business with regards to marriages and everything that is involved with these ceremonies. She enjoys it a lot, but as often with women, she loses herself in minor details, so she loses sight of the big picture. In other words, it is hardly profitable, but as long as she is having fun, I am not complaining.'

Hector had not noticed why Lex was laughing loudly, even overly hard, but his unpredictability was well known. The best thing was to laugh with him, which Hector did. When the laughter had died out, Hector inquired after the two children of Lex and Amélie.

'Lisa is now 24 and she is an instructor at a sailing school in Venice. I do not talk to her often and it looks like she does not mind. She has her own life there and of course she earns far too little to provide for her living, so I help her out every month.'

Hector expected another burst of laughter from Lex, but that did not happen this time. Lex further told him about his son Mars, who studied law at a university in the Netherlands. It appeared to Hector that his son was the apple of his eye, because when Lex talked about him he was full of praise. He also mentioned that his son was enthusiastically engaging in rowing competitions through his student corps, and that he was successful at it. So his children still engaged in water sports, which was not surprising because they had grown up with it. Lex had inherited the classic wooden sailing yacht from his father, which got admiring views in the marina of Ostend, and with which they used to make long journeys as a family. Lex leaned forward unexpectedly.

'But let's talk about your son now,' he said, and he looked at his guest intently.

This surprised Hector, and he took a sip of coffee first.

'After his technical science studies, my son, Daan, set up a small company from the campus, and this has taken a rapid growth. It is now a company with around 30 employees and is located on an industrial estate near Brussels. He specializes in batteries; their usage is growing rapidly due to the electronic revolution. It

concerns, for example, batteries in electric cars, bicycles, trucks and sport planes, but also in all other conceivable applications. He has the wind in his sails, and he estimated as much from his studies. He has great plans for the further growth of his company and he has drawn up a solid business plan for this. He needs 5 million euros to make his dream come true and he has now received 1.1 million via Moneytron, but it is still somewhat behind the expectations for achieving his goal of 5 million.'
Hector had emphatically mentioned the crowdfunding platform Moneytron, because he knew that Lex was closely involved in this. Lex pressed his index fingers and his thumbs against each other, which was a usual hand pose for the Freemasons. Outside the order, the sign of recognition was virtually unknown, but if you paid attention to it, the brothers who usually held high public functions could easily be recognized. You saw them in almost every news show on TV.

'I am not surprised about the 1.1 million, nor about the fact that it is stagnating,' Lex said. 'It originates from the three F's.'
Hector was not familiar with the expression 'the three F's' and asked him what it meant.

'Friends, Fools and Family,' Lex replied, and again he laughed uncontrollably loud.
Hector looked uncomfortable and decided not to join the outrageously loud laughter of his host this time.

'But seriously now,' Lex said when he had finished laughing, 'I had a quick look at your son's plans and immediately saw what is wrong with it. Lithium is still indispensable for the manufacture of batteries and your son needs a lot of it. There is no guaranteed supply of this important raw material in his plans. It comes mainly from the United States and now with those crazy trade wars, the question is whether the European Union will impose a tax of 30 percent or more on imports. Apart from the possibly higher price that has to be paid for it, it remains to be seen whether your son can even get the intended supplies. If they want to make things difficult for him, he might not receive anything. Therefore, he must be able to show that the deliveries of lithium are guaranteed for one hundred percent at a normal fixed price. Only then will it not be long before he reaches the 5 million euros. He could even earn more than that.'

Hector was surprised at Lex' sharp analysis that he had made from a superficial assessment. He could not think of any objections.

'But,' Lex continued, 'coincidentally - and coincidence does not exist by the way - I have a friend who owns a small island in the Pacific where significant amounts of lithium have recently been discovered in the ground. I can make sure that your son never has to worry about delivery and the price of lithium.'

'And are you prepared to do this?' Hector asked.

'Yes, my fellow, on certain conditions.'

Hector had not expected anything else and while his host refilled his cup with coffee, he was waiting anxiously to hear what the conditions would be.

'It's like this,' Lex said, 'about ten years ago we talked extensively about a campaign to put a wild park in the spotlight through free publicity, so that it would attract more visitors. You acted as my spokesman toward the park management and made a proposal for a promotional campaign, which entailed that three employees would dress up like Dutch police officers and hand out leaflets in the center of Antwerp with the warning that lions had escaped. The park agreed and carried out the promotional campaign, but they had not counted on one casual tourist being a real Dutch police officer, who did not appreciate the fact that he received a flyer with the official logo of the Dutch police. His Belgian colleagues arrested the trio and released them from their cell after a few hours. Only a small message appeared in the media, and it did not have the desired effect. An increase in the number of visitors did not happen and in retrospect, of course, it was not such a clever idea. I regard it as a good experience for a new action that really has to be clever. And for this, I need your help again.'

Hector had not seen this coming. He still remembered vividly this past campaign. He had cooperated in order to get higher in the hierarchy of the order, so that he could expand his network, and that would always yield more money. He did however, not benefit from it and remained an apprentice.

'What are you thinking of?' he asked.

'Let's analyze the mistakes we've made. In the first place, insiders of the park could trace back the action to you and me, and this cannot be the case this time. The staff cannot know anything about it. Secondly, we did not make use of the deliberate creation of fake news, something many people have become very good at now. It must therefore be something that has a big impact and that is not recognizable as fake. How you elaborate on this is up to you, I do not want to have anything to do with it, nor do I want to know. Of course, I hope to be able to recognize it when the event has taken place.' Hector lightly pursed his lips, from which Lex understood that he wanted to know what was in it for him.

'Of course I will help your son get the lithium in the desired quantity and at a fixed price, so I can guarantee you that he will make that 5 million. You will also be promoted to master in our order if the action has been successful, and by this, I mean that the number of visitors to the park will increase considerably. So, what do you say?'

'Do you have a budget in mind for this?' Hector asked. It turned out this was not the case. Hector would have to pay all costs out of his own pocket, and he would later be rewarded fairly.

'I trust you one hundred percent,' Hector said, 'but what guarantees do I have that what you promise will become a reality?'

'Normally, my fee for raising money for crowdfund-projects is five percent of the money invested,' Lex said. 'In this case, I will refrain from that and to show you that I will keep my promises, tomorrow you will see on the website that three anonymous people have each invested two tons in the project. This alone gives a positive incentive to the acquisition.'

Hector weighed his chances. He had no idea how he would shape the promotion, but all considering, his risk was limited, if he handled it smartly.

'Deal,' Hector said, and he reached out his hand. 'As soon as I see the extra six ton in the books, I start the assignment.'

Lex took his hand and he wished Hector every success. Lex stood up as a sign that the conversation had ended.

'I have some work to finish here, so I will not escort you to the door. Charles will wait for you downstairs.'

Hector left the room and Lex made three phone calls with investors who had already earned a lot of money, thanks to him. The conversations were short, and afterwards, Lex scurried around the seating area like a Geisha three times, then to the door, where he turned around and did the same six times. After completing his compulsory neurosis nine times, he left the room.

Chapter 3

Hector saw in his rear-view mirror the impressive castle getting smaller and smaller while he thought feverishly about his assignment. He had just witnessed a high-level chess game for which he was no match. You had to admire the way Lex arranged his affairs just like that, and the only thing he expected in return were shares in the lithium island. This way the aristocrat hit several birds with one stone. Hector belonged to the lower nobility and had always had to work hard for his money as well as take risks. The games the higher nobility played fascinated him and Lex was a master in it, just like his function within the brotherhood. Lex made his name twenty years ago when he averted a great danger. On that day, he was working as the master at Chateau des Amerois, the home of the order in Muno on the Belgian-French border. In the 19th century, the chateau was the birthplace of the first king of Belgium and now the headquarters of every royal, political leader, top industrialist, and banker who adhered to Satanism. Hector thought they were scary because of the way they behaved in private and out of sight of cameras. It was one of the reasons why he did not attend events of the order for years. To get ahead in life, it was useful not to get in their way and if possible, become friends with them. Lex' main feat was that he managed to make Marc Dutroux go away when he showed up at the chateau on the day of his escape. Dutroux had been studying his file in the court of

Neufchateau that morning. He overpowered one of his guards and captured his pistol. He stole a car to get away and five thousand Belgian agents were hunting him down. The only safe place for him was Chateau des Amerois as the bulwark from which he received his orders, for which he was later convicted. The master of the chateau prevented the castle from becoming a point of interest and the whole domain from being searched with a fine-tooth comb. The problems for the brotherhood would have been enormous if the complex under the castle had been discovered. Lex had informed Dutroux that he had to leave as quickly as possible, and that in return, he and his then wife, Michelle Martin, would be released early, as was later the case for his now ex-wife. In that respect, Lex had kept his word and Dutroux was supported in his requests for pardon so he would be freed from his imprisonment for life. Dutroux was stopped by a forester two kilometers outside the fences of Chateau des Amerois, and although he was carrying a loaded gun, Dutroux had not offered any resistance. Lex had quickly received the title of grandmaster as a reward for his bold and intelligent action.

After he had considered all this, Hector phoned his son, Daan, from his car. Daan answered his call almost immediately.

'Hello, son,' Hector said. 'I was just visiting somebody who can help you get that five million.'

'Oh really!' his son exclaimed. 'That would be nice.'

'Yes, and I am hopeful that it will actually work, but as always, there are conditions attached to it, which I would like to discuss with you. The person I spoke to will ensure that you have the lithium available for your plans, and at a fixed, normal price. Of course, he wants to see something in return. That means that he asks for five percent on the deposit that is still missing and you still have 3.9 million to go, so you can calculate how much.' Hector heard the tapping on a calculator and his son told him that it amounted to 195,000 euros.

'That will not be a problem, Dad,' Daan said. 'I have already taken this into account in my plans, so it does not hurt me. Did he or she have further requirements?'

'No, only that the payment of his fee goes through me. He wants to remain anonymous at all cost.'

'Good deal, Dad, you are the best! I assume that if we do not reach the five million, the whole plan will not go forth, and there is no question that I have to pay any fee.'

'Of course, and maybe you'll get even more money,' Hector said, and they finished their phone conversation. The father was very satisfied with himself and had just created a large budget, which he could use for the action commissioned by the grandmaster. His objective was to use as little as possible, so that his profit was as big as possible. He had to pre-finance it, but he had enough cash for that. 'What you can do, I can too, Lex,' Hector muttered, and a wide grin appeared on his face.

Chapter 4

The next morning, before anything else, Hector checked the Moneytron website for the latest state of affairs. He immediately phoned his son.

'Have you seen it yet?' he asked when his son answered his call.

'What?'

'Moneytron.'

'No, not yet, Dad, but I'm going there now. Whaaat! Is this the latest score of the money that is invested in the project!' he exclaimed. '1.7 million euros, wow, this is how we get there!'

'Didn't I tell you, son?'

'Yeees, but is there something I should do? How do we go from here?'

Hector told him that he just had to wait and that if there was news that could awaken the interest of other investors, they would discuss it. Hector heaved a deep sigh after the telephone conversation. 'It giet oan,' he said to himself, an expression used to announce that the Friesian Elfstedentocht, the 11 City Skating Race, went through. He still had no idea how he would handle it. He lacked inspiration, and searched the internet for remarkable things about zoos and similar institutions. Soon he came across a movie about a male dolphin that was sexually satisfied by a caregiver in a dolphinarium. Hector thought it was shocking. He quickly searched further and found the silverback gorilla, Bokito, who had escaped from his enclosure in Blijdorp in 2007. First, the ape had seized a woman and bitten her a hundred times over her entire body. He had dragged her through the bushes, severely injuring her hand, which later turned out to be shattered. Then the gorilla walked to the zoo restaurant, where he destroyed a glass door and made three more victims, slightly injured this time, including a man in a wheelchair. The zoo staff compelled Bokito into a corner and stunned him with a gun. It was big news on the exact day of the 150th anniversary of the zoo. The international press was also interested in the film footage that restaurant guests made that day when Bokito was still there, although it was not very spectacular. The still young male gorilla showed no more aggressive behavior, but panic had spread through the park and the park was evacuated and closed for visitors for the rest of the day. Bokito had earlier escaped from his enclosure in a zoo in Berlin in 2004, but that time there had been no injuries. Later, the woman who was attacked first confessed that Bokito was her favorite and she paid a visit to Blijdorp especially for him three times a week. She stated that she had built up a relationship with Bokito with the safety glass in between them. The whole world judged her and she was accused of being utterly insane, until an evolutionary biologist and former professor defended her in the press. He reduced it to normal behavior of apes. Bokito wanted her in his harem. It brought grist to the mill of the zoo, because it generated 50,000 extra visitors that year, making Blijdorp the best-visited zoo in the Netherlands in 2007. In 2016, the park started a merchandise line with Bokito mugs, a game and things like lunch boxes with his image. Nine years after the incident the gorilla was still immensely popular.

Hector calculated what it had yielded by multiplying the number of extra visitors by the average spending, which he estimated at twenty-five euros per person. The result was € 1,250,000 which was serious money, and if Lex only owned 10 percent of the shares, it would yield him around 100,000 € after deduction of direct costs. Cumulatively, perhaps half a million euros. Hector imagined that he or someone else would release a lion between the visitors in the freely accessible part of the wildlife park that Lex had referred to. This might result in more casualties than Bokito and deaths might not be prevented. According to Hector, such irrevocable victims were not very tempting to new visitors. The park would have a lot of trouble, he assumed, but on the other hand, maybe it would not matter. People had a thirst for sensation, as some sort of primal urge, and the commotion would not be less because of it. Nevertheless, he decided that deadly victims should be prevented as much as possible. Blijdorp had compensated all serious claims and the Public Prosecution had seen no reason for criminal prosecution, it would have been different if there had been deaths. In that case, the animal would have undoubtedly been shot so there would have been nothing left to visit. If Hector wanted to succeed in his action, a dangerous animal would have to break loose, but how could he manage that? The wildlife park was full of cameras and nowadays everybody had photo and film equipment at the ready as well as a device to go online immediately. The influence of social media had increased considerably since 2007, with all the associated peripheral phenomena. The chance that Hector or an accomplice would be caught when they opened a fence was fundamental and he knew that the game park was well protected. For the time being, he did not have the solution, but he had already found a direction for his nefarious plan. Only the details had yet to be completed. For days on end, he continued to study the wildlife park, especially the freely accessible parts. He mapped it out for himself in detail and was able to find his way blindly in the virtual park. That was the preliminary work, but he had to visit the wildlife park himself, because this was only a schematic study beforehand. Twice he visited the wildlife park and paid close attention to the habits of the staff and he read everything he could find about the park. After a week, he woke up in the middle of the night. The solution had come to him like a vision. The animals did not have to break out, but visitors had to break in and go inside the fence. He made a note of it on the notepad that he found in the drawer of his bedside table. Hector had found the key to his success.

Chapter 5

In the Northeast of Moldova, in the town of Soroca, the gypsy Malev Rotari was sitting in the doorway of his caravan. He held up a banknote of 20 Moldavian leu. He looked attentively at the note in the pale interior lighting of his trailer. The exchange rate of the note was one euro. The 15th century fort that was depicted on the note was the same fort Malev was looking at now. The five high towers, four of them with a round roof, and the tower above the entrance with a square roof, stood about two hundred meters away from him in the beautiful atmospheric light spread by the floodlights. The monument, built in the round design, was the pride of Moldova and an important tourist attraction. Stephen the Great, the voivode of Moldavia, had it built during his reign from the year 1457 to 1504 as a fortification to prevent Ottoman Turks from conquering and plundering the country. Stephan won the Battle of Vaslui that took place in 1475. He received the honorary title of Athleta Christi, a high award given to him by Pope Sixtus IV. To this day, Stephen the Great is still honored as a national hero in Moldova.

Malev, who never before studied the banknote so extensively, rolled it up in the bundle of notes that he kept together with a rubber band. He put it in his trouser pocket and grabbed the beer bottle, which he had held upright between his feet on the wire-iron step. He drank greedily until it was empty and threw it carelessly under the caravan. His circus had settled in Soroca that morning, and he and his entire family had worked hard to turn the round courtyard of the fort into an arena. The steep stands were built from scaffolding material and wooden planks with seats for about 300 visitors. If all these seats were taken, they could place people in the upper section, which had been restored and finished in 2012. Behind its robust balustrade, there were seats for another two hundred people. The construction of the arena was going to be the task for the next day. The first show was already planned for the next evening, so they were on a tight schedule to finish everything on time. In the corner of his eye, he saw a ship on the Dniester River that he recognized from the sidelights as the customs patrol ship on the border river between Moldova and Ukraine.

The courtyard of the fort was far from smooth and he had been struggling to find a way to lay down a flat, supported floor without damaging it. According to him, it would not be strong enough for the elephants, so he decided in advance that this part of the program was cancelled. The elephants would only fulfill their promotional function in a trunk-to-tail procession through the city to let everyone know that the circus had arrived. Malev had traveled a lot with the circus in his life. From the Algarve in the south of Portugal to the highlands of Scotland, and from Estonia to deep inside of Turkey and everything in between. It had been a hard life and in many of these places, they had not attracted enough visitors. In the family, however, there was no regret about this, because the creativity in smuggling drugs had been elevated to an art in order to absorb the losses. Customs personnel were not so keen to inspect the lion cages for drugs during transport and if a fanatical officer with ambitious plans for his career still insisted on it, they released a lion - on a leash or not - for a few minutes, which caused enough commotion to give their career plans a lower priority. Malev thoroughly enjoyed watching the bombastic plays the customs officers performed, after which, they begged for the lion to be put back into his cage as quickly as possible. Malev was never caught for smuggling, only for small thefts, extortion, and fights. That was part of their rough life from the olden days, and when it came down to it, they lived up to their reputation, just as many people expected from them due to the prejudice toward his people. The family members were very social toward each other within the framework of the closed family. The clan was praised and feared until Malev was tired of working out acquittals for his family members, with or without the help of lawyers. Because of all the skirmishes, it became more and more difficult to negotiate rights to pitch their tent, no matter how much Malev was prepared to pay. At one point, he had enough and decided to handle matters differently. The circus changed its name and there was no more smuggling. Disturbances were out of the question and money laundering had taken over as the new creed. They kept thorough records of the income and expenditure, in which they fiddled with the visitor numbers as well as the amount of performances. Criminals liked to use Malev's money laundering plant, but the circus had slowly withered over the years. The paying visitors decreased considerably in number while the costs kept rising. The deathblow had been the hated European Union, who no longer tolerated working with wild animals. That is why Malev had withdrawn to his native country and they now only travelled through the surrounding countries, where wild animals in the circus were still allowed. It limited their range, but Malev liked it that way. His corpulent body was almost spent and with his sixty-five years, he wanted to live much more quietly. His granddaughter, who was responsible for the administration and promotion, was standing a bit further, talking with the jugglers while they were practicing their acts. She waved at him when her eyes met his and she gestured him near her. Malev raised his thumb and stood up to get another bottle of beer from his fridge.

'Salute pipopadre,' she said cheerfully as always. She stepped into the caravan and sat down at the oval table. Malev always laughed at her and he put a bottle of beer in front of her, which she popped by putting her finger in it, and then pulled it out crookedly, which caused a popping sound. It belonged to the worldwide etiquette of drinking beer from a bottle, but nobody understood the meaning of it. It was an unwritten habit. Clinking the bottles against each other completed the ritual.

'Nastrovja,' she said, and both took a sip.

'How is the ticket sale going?' Malev asked.

'Very good,' his granddaughter beamed.

She opened her folder and showed him the leaflet that they had distributed in hotels and lodgings in the area. Also among conductors and bus drivers. Merchants in the poor area had bought discount tickets for resale. Months earlier, she had built a website on which the circus was announced with an English translation. Booking the fort as a circus location had been an excellent idea. They spent a week in Soroca with matinee and evening performances. She made a rough estimate of the expected total turnover and she calculated they would at least make 15,000 euros if every ticket cost 100 Moldovan leu, or 5 euros. Children up to 12 years went for half the price.

'You did very well, Milena,' Malev said.

The granddaughter glowed and rattled on and on that, there was much interest in the liger, Mira. Mira was the result of crossing a tiger and a lion. In nature, these two did not meet, but in their circus, it had happened. The genetic manipulation had proceeded naturally and had produced a cub that eventually became two and a half times larger than her parents were. It was a spectacular animal and an attraction. Mira was a sweetheart and it was not very difficult to teach her tricks. The

29

disadvantage was that she ate twenty-five kilos of meat a day.

'I think the entrance fee for the local population is rather high,' she said, 'but there is not that much to do in this corner of the world. We depend on tourists and Moldovans who can afford it.'

'You can still vary the admission price with the pitches in the upper gallery,' Malev said, 'but I'll leave that to you. You're clever enough to figure it out.'

He winked at her to confirm his words.

The stable master knocked at the caravan and the grandchild stood up. She gave her grandfather a loving hug and left the caravan. Again, bottles were opened, popped, and clinked. Malev discussed the performances and the order of the acts with the stable master.

'The elephants stay outside and the trapeze number cannot take place here either,' Malev said. 'I have looked for a safe way to make the trapeze work, but I am cancelling the act. It is too dangerous in the open air with the possible influence of the wind, and besides that, the swing length does fit in the limited interior space of the fort.'

'OK,' the stable master said. 'I'll solve that with a human pyramid, extra jokes and antics from the clowns, and an act with horses, combined with Jack Russells.'

Chapter 6

Slowly, Hector made all pieces of the puzzle fit together. He had written out the main lines for himself on a piece of paper. The list boiled down to no deadly victims, and if possible, no wounded either. It had to be a bizarre and unfathomable sight to see. It should leave no traces and be spontaneously filmed by a casual visitor to the wildlife park. Such a thing would undoubtedly end up on the internet and if it were idiotic enough, it would generate millions of views and a lot of discussion, which was indispensable for a thorough and successful campaign. 'And Bob is your uncle,' Hector laughed, subdued from behind his desk in his stuffy study. He began to see the fun of it and asked himself who would be willing to take a walk between dangerous four-legged predators. He thought of people who were used to working with such animals. Animal trainers, who knew exactly how to deal with them. The profession of lion tamer no longer existed in Western Europe. Animal activists, supported by the European Union, had ruled out the profession, but he knew that it still existed in countries that had not yet joined the EU. He had an image in his mind from Romania - of a bear with a ring through his nose. The animal did not have a good life, but as long as he provided money for his boss, who was likely some sad beggar, this situation would remain for a long time in those regions. Romania was a starting point for Hector and on the internet. He was looking for itinerant circuses,

31

but could not find what he was looking for. Romania had been a part of the European Union since 2007, when the country lost its naivety towards Western Europe. They made lots of money there now. His eye fell on Moldova, the small country east of Romania that was wedged between Romania and Ukraine. Hector knew nothing about Moldova, but he remembered that he had seen their entries for the Eurovision Song Contest. He could not even locate the country on the world map. It was a republic where some 3.5 million people lived in an area slightly larger than Belgium. It used to be a province of the Soviet Union but became independent in 1991. A strong urbanization had not yet taken place and the majority of the population still lived in rural areas. The main religion was Catholic Romanian-Russian orthodox, and the Islamic faith was not practiced in the country. Moldova, the poorest country in Europe, imported a lot and exported little. The roads were appalling and the tourists were advised not to go on public roads after sunset. The roads in the country were moderately to downright bad and unlit vehicles such as horse and wagon were still very common. Agriculture and cattle raising were on an equal footing in Moldova. Tourism was still underdeveloped, but it was on the rise due to low prices and friendly people. The average annual income of a working person was € 2,750 per person per year. Hector was immediately happy about it, because if he found what he was looking for, the rest of the job would be cushy. After all, who would not be prepared to double the annual income in one blow at a low risk? In his fervent enthusiasm about the country that he had already closed in his heart, he googled circuses and found exactly what he was looking for. They gave circus performances in an old renovated fortress in the town of Soroca, in northeast Moldova. The photo of the liger who looked at him from the screen with his big friendly face, made his heart jump in his chest. He checked when the circus would give their performances and to his relief, this had been just an announcement in advance. The first performance would take place in about a week and he read everything about it that he could find. He was pleased to note that the owners of the circus were gypsies.

Through a hotel-booking website, Hector immediately booked a room for a week for only 31 euros per day. Hotel Central was a top-notch accommodation according to the reviews. The hotel took good care of hygiene and it had a very good restaurant, if the comments about it were true. It had Wi-Fi, TV, airco, and it was only a 10-minute walk from the fort. For the time being, he did not put too much trust in the reviews, since he knew that they were often made by the hotel itself, and because some of the assessments could not be made by a Dutch speaker. They were full of crooked sentences and mistakes. It seemed that the texts had been put through a translation machine without a care and had not been checked. He did not need to apply for a visa for Moldova. His passport was sufficient and he booked a direct flight from Brussels to the capital, Chisinau. He would still be 200 kilometers away from his final destination, but he would bridge that distance with a rental car. A thrill of excitement went through his body as if he were on a voyage of discovery to a far and unknown land. Prior to his journey, he still had to prepare everything in detail, but a whole week was long enough for that.

Chapter 7

Malev was glad that he had arranged a boom hoist to lower large square bags of sand from above into the piste where the staff poured out the fine-grained sand. Then they distributed the sand evenly over the floor. If they had to use wheelbarrows that day for this whole job, they would not have been ready on time. The boom lift was a considerable expense, and in a week from now, he would have to spend that money again to remove the sand in the same way. Soroca would be a great success for the circus. There was no longer any doubt about this, and his granddaughter had already proposed to have extra shows for the schools of Soroca and those from the neighboring villages and towns. That did not yield as much as an ordinary performance, but it would not hurt now that they were here. If everything went smoothly without squabbles, Malev could add this event to his calendar every year. It would put Soroca on the map and was something the members of the city council were very receptive. For the premiere, the entire board and their close relatives were invited, and they would get special seats. Malev knew better than anyone did about how important these people were, but he did not have a high opinion of them anyway.

There was a hustle and bustle around the fort. Everyone was busy to get the last details just right. They rolled out a wide, red carpet in front of the entrance and copper-colored poles, connected with a thick rope, were placed on both sides of it. Frenzied children rushed to and fro. The ecstasy was clearly visible from their faces and people from outside flocked together in front of the cages with the lions and tigers. Two hours before the first performance, there was a queue in front of the ticket booth and the seats were already sold out. Now people eagerly bought the tickets for the pitches. It was a long time since the circus had so many visitors and Malev regarded it as the crown of his life's work. Trays with sandwiches were handed around for the employees of the circus and after the show, a barbecue would be held in the courtyard surrounded by a circle of caravans. They did not want any prying eyes and the screens between the caravans would prevent that.

It was a fortress and that meant that everything had to go through the main entrance, including not only the public, but also the artists and the animals. Stefanus the Great had not taken this type of use into account and there were no emergency exits. The commander of the local fire service thought the situation was questionable. However, even before he issued a negative advisory, he had been silenced by the mayor of Soroca. The complimentary tickets for the commander and his family compensated his earlier grievances.

Two hours later, the entire audience had found a place to sit or stand. The performance was sold out. Spotlights moved wildly in different colors across the audience, of which, the families with small children sat in the first rows. There was already a great atmosphere and this was whipped up even further by loud music, comparable to the blaring loudspeakers of the bumper cars at a fairground. The focus of the searchlights shifted to the entrance where a red curtain was parted in the middle by someone with a deadly pale face. The person stuck his head and the upper half of his body through the curtain. A black tear dangled beneath his left eye. He wore a pointed hat of red felt.

'Pierot, Pierot, Pierot,' the children shrieked, and bewildered, the clown disappeared, which led to great laughter among the highly honored audience. The performance had begun.

Chapter 8

Early in the morning, Hector landed at the airport in
Chisinau, picked up his rental car, and drove to the
border town in the far north as fast as he could. He
passed the landscape of vast fields and enormous
vineyards, and the farther north he got, the hillier the
surroundings became. At first, he did not notice the
quality of the roads, but this changed when he came
farther north. He had to be alert and react quickly to pits
in the road and missing asphalt. It took him five hours to
get to the destination and before he checked in at the
hotel, he first bought a ticket for the circus. He tried to
absorb as much as possible of what he saw and to pay
attention to things that could later be of benefit to him. A
friendly young woman with blonde, long hair was sitting
in the tollbooth next to the entrance to the fort. Her long
blonde hair was adorned with colorful tresses in various
colors. Normally, Hector's first thought was that if he had
such colors in his hair, he would have it dyed, despite the
fact that he was bald. In this setting, though, he thought
the colors were fitting. Thankfully, he received the ticket
after his payment of 100 leu and he put it away in his
wallet. He attended the first performance that evening
and he would do the same in the coming days, even twice
a day. In order to get as little attention as possible, he
would buy a ticket every day, because it would look
weird if he bought tickets for thirteen performances at
once. Such a thing was, of course, unusual. He wanted to

get a good view of everything first before he approached them. His mission was simple and clear, but he had to consider everything. He did not want, nor could he afford a failure.

He watched the construction of the circus with great interest, as far as he could see. A boom lift dropped one sandbag after another into the courtyard of the impressive fort, of which he caught a glimpse through an open curtain. He walked around as inconspicuously as possible, paying attention to who was working for the circus and how they behaved. His first conclusion was that they were hard workers and he imagined that he would see these people again in the evening, but would not recognize them because of their costumes. Hector knew that Soroca was the gipsy capital of Moldova and in the Roma quarter, rich families had built pompous houses looking like the Capitol in Washington. They had made their fortune in particular in the textile industry, but since the bottom had fallen out of this, many suffered poverty like in the past. The villas were uninhabited except for a gypsy king, and the other gypsies lived in their shabby little cottages. The men at the circus had the typical appearance of Roma gypsies.

The circus was a big event in the town of 40,000 inhabitants. This became immediately clear to Hector. There was an atmosphere of excitement, but that could also be his own projection. He could not remember if his parents or grandparents had ever taken him to a circus.

The only thing he remembered was the Russian state circus, of which performances were shown on the TV around Christmas. Hector walked around the fort and through the surrounding park. A few times, he sat down on a bench to look around at the area. He did the same at the river with the entrance to the fort at his back. For the time being, he had seen enough and he decided to check in at Hotel Central, which he had found quickly. The hotel was fairly new and modern, and it could easily withstand the comparison with the standard to which he was accustomed. The hall with the reception looked fresh, functional, and colorful. The receptionist was very friendly and she informed him extensively in understandable German-English-French. She took all the time she needed, as nobody was waiting behind him. She also told him about the sights in the town. The hotel had an indoor swimming pool built in Gothic style, which Hector had overlooked when booking. It had been a long time since he had been swimming and the pool looked inviting, but he did not have swimming trunks in his luggage. He told the receptionist this in an equal mixture of languages and she came with a solution. She showed him a few models from which he made a choice. The purchase was billed against his room number and a liftboy in an old-fashioned uniform brought him and his luggage to his room. Hector rewarded the nice young man with a 20-leu note. The room was traditionally decorated with old but well-maintained functional furniture, and as far as Hector was concerned, it was indeed clean. Even the lid of the drain in the shower was shining. The hotel turned out to be a good choice for him and after unpacking his luggage, he took a French and an English newspaper under his arm, as he had not found the time to read the news. In the restaurant section, he chose a table at the window and he read the articles that he normally did not pay attention to, and after a second cup of coffee, his attention was drawn by a sound that he did not recognize until three elephants walked past his window. The parade was accompanied by loud music, acrobats on stilts, four clowns, and jugglers who showed their skills. At the end of the short procession, a horse pulled a flat cart with a cage on top, in which a surly lion was looking ahead. He hardly moved. Hector thought the male lion might have been drugged, because if he was alert, and possibly broke out, it could lead to victims. That would generate a lot of publicity.

'The circus is in town,' a waiter said as he walked to the window. Hector saw a glint in his eyes.

Chapter 9

'Salute pipopadre,' Malev's granddaughter said on the fourth evening when she brought him the moneybox with the daily turnover, as she did every day. As a precaution, Malev closed the curtains of his caravan. He had been robbed once and the experience was one he did not want to repeat. The perpetrators would definitely not repeat their action, because after his family members tracked them down and beat them to a pulp, they buried them in a deep hole.

Triumphantly, she placed stacks of banknotes, bundled per currency, on the table and took a sip from her bottle of beer.

'71, 120 leu,' she said, and gave him a note with the numbers.

Malev was very satisfied and looked at the back of the note on which the total turnover was stated and her adjusted expectation. After the premiere - that was completely sold out - the number of visitors had decreased, but there were always so many visitors that the upper gallery was used at every performance. The entire Soroca event was expected to generate around 23,000 euros in turnover and the possible additional performances had not even been taken into account yet. Everything had gone perfectly until now, and Malev had submitted an application to extend the stay of the circus in the city for two more days, but he had not yet received the green light from the city council. Malev gathered the piles of money together and put them in his safe under the sink, as well as the bag of coins that was handed to him.

'Something bothers me,' she said after the vault was closed with a rattling twist on the combination lock. Malev looked at her questioningly.

'What is it?'

'Well, ever since the premiere, there is a bald man in the audience who seems to be taking notes. That is rather suspicious. I had him followed and it turns out he is staying here in the city in Hotel Central. We do not yet know what his nationality is, but I suspect he is a German. In Chisinau, he rented a car that he used to get here. We know that because there is a sticker on the windshield of his car with the logo of the rental company and also the rental location, namely, the airport of Chisinau.'

Malev reacted as if he had been stung by a wasp and he cursed loudly.

'Why would a German take the trouble to come all the way here and watch one show after another,' he said. 'Of course, it could be someone with a sexual deviation, who gets horny from circuses and everything that has to do with it, but he could also be from the tax authorities or worse still, from a secret service. If he is a secret agent, he is a very clumsy one, because we would not have been on to him if he were any good. What do you think his intentions are?'

She shrugged and told him she had no idea. Malev did not like the fact that someone carefully followed his circus and even took notes about it. It was not in Malev's nature to wait patiently to find out what the reason was. He lived with the credo that attack was better than defense.

'If he appears again tomorrow afternoon and also tomorrow evening, then I want to talk to that little man and we will find out what he is doing here. I do not want any trouble, because that might jeopardize the extra shows, and who knows, it could be something serious and then we may have to forget about this event in the future.'

Meanwhile, Hector had built a good relationship with the hotel staff and he was in the best mood. Another reason for joy was that his son had informed him that he had been approached by someone who owned an island that was full of lithium. He had signed an agreement for long-term purchase of the stuff at a normal fixed rate. This would also be communicated on the Moneytron profile page. Daan was euphoric about the deal and he saw a golden future ahead of him. Hector was just as enthusiastic about it, and for him, this was the second confirmation that Lex kept his word. However, it increased the pressure on his shoulders, because now it was important that he also kept to the appointments.

44

He had already visited seven performances of the circus and he was not disappointed in the quality of what they offered. It could not be compared to the Russian state circus, but the level was higher than what he expected initially. It was a classic circus with all the characteristics that belonged to it. In a performance of almost two hours, all acts followed each other quickly. Regularly, they took someone from the audience to take part in some element of the show. It always led to hilarity, but they ensured that the 'victim' could always leave the arena with their head held high. The circus artists themselves burst with pleasure during their shows, and this appealed to Hector. The clowns in particular knew how to get the laugh of the audience on their side with their jokes and antics during the switching of acts. It was at a high level of improvisation, so that Hector himself also regularly laughed. It seemed like everything happened spontaneously, which of course was only partly so. For Hector it was art with a capital A, and he was sorry that it was doomed to extinction in the rest of Europe. Hector enjoyed how the children in the first rows were entertained. He got a lump in his throat from this bygone form of touching, joyful and pure amusement. The children had the time of their lives, and Hector wondered whether West-European children would also react so spontaneously, as they were often hardly prepared to leave their tablets for a while.

45

At about three quarters of the show, staff ran into the arena with the parts of the cage for the lions and the tigers. The clowns interfered with it and that led to funny situations, which made it uncertain whether the colossus would ever be set up, but then - as in a giant origami - the cage was erected and the access tunnel for the wild animals set in position. The animal trainers, and in particular a young, athletically built woman, could make the lions and tigers do all kinds of tricks. It did not lead to dangerous situations in the performances that Hector visited, and if it ever did, then two snipers were there who could intervene. They did not take their eyes off the performance. If necessary, they had rifles with anesthesia within their reach. The highlight of this part of the performance was the liger Mira. The huge beast had the withers height of a pony. Hector had never seen one before. It was a sweetheart who liked to be cuddled and they could do incredible tricks with her. The blonde lion tamer even rode on her back. Then the animals were quickly escorted away and the cage taken down. Once again, all artists entered the arena to receive the overwhelming applause from the audience, who were standing on the benches. The clapping, whistling and cheering persisted for a long time, and in an elated mood, the audience left the fort. It was not over yet, because as soon as everyone was outside, the show ended with impressive fireworks. Hector enjoyed another nice evening on the fourth day of his stay in Soroca. He stood with his back to the river and in front of him, was the elated audience who were delighted at the sight of the fireworks.

Hector felt something being pushed against his side and he looked into the eyes of a slender man next to him who looked scary with long sticky hair and a stubby face. The man had bad teeth with a golden tooth among his almost black top teeth.

'Mitkommen,' the man hissed between his teeth. Hector wanted to tear himself away, but the man held him tightly by his arm and Hector did not know what it was, but the pressure point in his side assumed painful proportions. If it was a gun with which he was threatened, he could be shot just like that. Nobody knew that he was in Moldova. His body would never be found. All of this went through his mind and he decided to cooperate and then see where he ended up. If it was a robbery, the robber could have all his possessions. Hector's life was much too dear to him.

Chapter 10

Hector's assailant led him along the crowd at a hefty pace. They walked towards the temporary gypsy camp, something Hector had not expected. He expected he would be dragged into the bushes where he would be robbed of his possessions, so he was kind of relieved. He had not yet figured out how to get into contact with the gypsies and now he was taken straight into their midst. About halfway, Hector stumbled, but the man who was still holding him tightly prevented him from falling and pulled him up with a jerk. Meanwhile, the man jovially greeted the people they met on their dimly lit path; apparently, he was a well-known person. Through a flap in the fence, they walked directly over the courtyard towards a darkened caravan. There was no one to be seen and they let Hector go first on the step and inside the caravan. Someone pushed him in the back which made him fall forward. He was caught by another man who looked equally unkempt. Hector had not noticed these men earlier in or around the circus. This one also had a golden tooth among his neglected teeth. Hector imagined that they were brothers. In the middle of the caravan stood a wooden armchair and in a harsh manner they made it clear to Hector that he had to sit down. Then they tied a rope around his waist and attached his wrists and ankles to the back and legs of the chair with tie rips. There was no way he could escape. His assailant put a short lead rod on the table, which was the thing that had poked him in his side all this time. Meanwhile, a third man had entered the caravan behind them and said something unintelligible to the brothers. The tooth devils withdrew and when they had closed the door of the caravan behind them, Hector was alone with a man who had a similar stature as him and who was bald as well, but he had to be at least ten years older than Hector. He was probably the head clown who was in charge of the other three, because he still had a bit of white make-up under his dark eyes. He took the lead bar off the table and stood threateningly in front of Hector. With his right hand, he tapped the rod in the palm of his other hand, and Hector expected to get a slap in his face at any moment.

'Was wollen Sie,' the man asked grimly.
Hector replied in German that he was looking for suitable circus artists for a performance, which he corrected in English. The man put the bar back on the table, opened Hector's short leather jacket, and reached for the inside pocket that held Hector's wallet. Attentively, the man looked at the contents and at Hector's passport.

'Tourist?' he asked and Hector nodded. Then the man pulled the notebook from the other inside pocket. He also studied this thoroughly and leafed through it. 'Was ist das?' the man asked and he held one of the text pages in front of Hector's face. Apparently, he could not read what it said and Hector felt a bit more secure now.

'It has to do with one of the shows,' Hector replied, adding that he had been preparing it for a while. Malev relaxed and wondered if it had been smart to meet a potential new customer in this manner. He sat down at the table.

'Sag mir,' he said.

'It's all about a perfect trick of the mind,' Hector said and he told him globally in English what the intention was, and when he got the impression that Malev did not understand, he translated it into German, in which he was less adept. When he had told his story, Malev asked him questions about how much time it would take, how many people were involved, and when it all had to take place. Hector gave him the answers and then asked if he could be released from the chair. His nose itched and he wanted to use his hands to rub away the discomfort. Malev apologized and cut Hector loose from the chair. He shook his hand and introduced himself as Malev Rotari. He then asked if his guest would like a beer. Hector was relieved and gladly accepted the offer. He did not need a glass.

'Wie viele?' Malev asked, moving his thumb and forefinger over each other, to make clear that he was talking about money.

'Ten thousand euros at the start, ten thousand euros when we begin at the wildlife park, and another ten thousand afterwards,' Hector said.
Malev did not move a muscle and quickly thought about this bizarre offer. Who, for God's sake, would want to spend so much money for something as simple as that? It

beat the turnover of the Soroca week and he felt that there was even more in it for him.

'Nein, nein, not enough by far,' he said with a slightly aggrieved expression on his face and he doubled the offer. After some haggling, they agreed to three times, 15,000 euros. The expenses, such as the travel and accommodation costs, were the loose change, and after Hector declared his willingness to assume responsibility, they sealed the deal with a firm handshake.

Hector outlined in detail for Malev what the intention was and said that it was very important that they had to use their improvisational talents at the time, something in which Hector had every confidence. He explicitly made it clear to Malev that the whole action should only be known to those directly involved. That never ever the truth should come to light. If all this succeeded, there would be more jobs in the future, which he said as a kind of guarantee to Malev who agreed to the deal. Malev, in turn, saw a new market open up for him and wondered to what extent it was punishable. He saw it as something that belonged to normal work for them.

Hector returned to the hotel in a cheerful mood, despite the initially precarious situation in which he had ended up. He had earned 150,000 euros that night, although he had not calculated the expenses yet. He could not blame Malev that he would have been prepared to pay double the amount. That would not have been in proportion to the effort it would take, but to the economic value that it represented. He agreed with Malev to meet each other every day after the last performance, something Hector was already looking forward to. The exciting circus life of gypsies exerted a great attraction on him. The atmosphere, the smell of animals and the enthusiastic audience, in short, the whole entourage, had aroused deep feelings in him, as in a childhood dream he had never had. Now that he was granted a look behind the scenes, he could experience the entire circus and give it a special place in his heart. He did not yet have grandchildren, but if he ever did, he would travel everywhere with them to give them this special feeling, no matter how far he had to travel.

He had already come up with a nickname for himself: 'grandpa circus'.

In his hotel room, he looked at his right side in the mirror and there was a black spot of a hematoma. The first trick of the mind had already taken place, because he would swear he had been kept under control with a pistol.

The following evenings, Hector visited Malev, and a friendship grew between them. Despite their big differences, they shared a passion: reading classics such as 'Anatevka' by Sjolem Alejchem, who wrote the book at the end of 19th century. They could talk for hours about that book alone and Malev had also read many Western books, but they had to work as well.

Chapter 11

Malev was delighted that it was no longer possible to
drive cars between the lions and the tigers in the wild
park. After many incidents, in which vehicles were
damaged, it was abolished ten years ago. Lions - even
though they were born in captivity - were much more
dangerous than the cheetahs Hector came up with.
Cheetahs in the wild survived by eating small animals,
and the men made the decision to use a small child to
lure the cheetahs towards them. The child had to be
accompanied and protected by an adult. The female lion
tamer was already on Hector's wish list as the most
important person for the job. She would be in charge, as
she was able to assess how the animals properly reacted.
For the role of the child, they decided on the lion tamer's
son who was four years old. They had to look as much as
possible like an inconspicuous company and that is why
they also wanted to use a niece of Malev, who was
twelve years old. Hector had noticed a nineteen-year-old
juggler because of his improvisational talent, so he was
also added to the group. With his posture, he could chase
away the cheetahs before they caught a child, something
that had already happened once in the park when a 10-
year-old child on his own was seized by a cheetah and
bitten in his arm. The child escaped with a fright, and the
park stated later that the warning signs might not have
been clear enough for everyone. Malev would coordinate
the entire mission and he would also be present in person,

but would remain invisible because he could possibly be recognized. After all, he had been wandering around in Western Europe for a long time. They talked extensively about safety, and in the end, they agreed to take a sniper of the circus with them, who could intervene with an anesthetic rifle if it got out of hand. His position had to be in another vehicle with a collapsible back seat so he could keep his rifle in position in the trunk. It was necessary to drill holes for the barrel and the visor in the rear of the car, and Hector had just the man for that, who could also restore the car back to its old state afterwards. Including the driver of the 'actors', they needed seven people.

'If it fails and we are arrested, then what?' Malev asked.

'Then it is just a family from Moldavia on vacation, who visit the wildlife park in German cars with false French license plates and who have no idea how dangerous it is to get close to cheetahs. In that case, they have to plead innocence and it will all blow over. They will think that the mother has put her child in danger, but youth care and judicial authorities have no jurisdiction in Moldova, so if it is maintained that it was a stupid action, with an apology, that will be the end of it. It is better not to be caught, of course, and that applies to you as the driver of the car in which the sniper is located. You and the shooter do not get out of the car, so they will not suspect you of anything,' Hector said.

'Wait a minute,' Malev said, 'German rental cars with false French number plates?'

'Yes,' Hector replied. 'You will fly to Cologne and rent two cars at the airport. Then you will drive to Reims in France in those cars and book a hotel there. I pick up the cars and have the number plates changed. In addition, the holes are drilled for the sniper. This will make it difficult to trace you and if they want an explanation about these French license plates, then you have to come up with a story, but in any case do not say anything, absolutely nothing, about this action. If they have nothing to charge you with, you will be deported and a punishment or penalty will be small, but as I said, it is more convenient not to be caught.'

'Okay, I understand,' Malev said, 'but the sniper needs a stun gun and it seems too conspicuous and too risky to smuggle it to Cologne by plane.'

'Good comment, Malev,' Hector said. 'Just give me the brand and the type number, and then I make sure that there is one in your rental car somewhere invisible to the naked eye. I think we will hide the weapon behind a screen in the door, but I'll let you know by then.'
Hector did not have to wait long for the brand and type number, because Malev took a rifle like the one he wanted, from his wardrobe. It was a Dan-inject double-barreled anesthetic rifle. A common weapon that was used all over the world to inactivate animals temporarily.

'It's easy to obtain in Western Europe,' Malev said. 'You do not need a gun permit and anyone over eighteen can shoot with it, formally only under the supervision of a veterinarian and with the permission of a local police chief. Blah blah blah...'

It became clear to Hector that in Moldova the rules for possessing and using such a gun were different. According to him, if the worst came to the worst, there was not always a veterinarian around, in Moldova or anywhere else on the globe, and there was no immediate permission from a chief constable. Such a weapon was only used in case of emergency and served to protect someone. If a lot of paperwork was needed afterwards, then they would deal with it then, but not at the moment that the tranquilizer was shot. Hector took the gun from Malev and looked at it attentively. For him it was just a rifle, but a connoisseur would laugh at him.

'It will be OK, Malev. I'll take care of it,' Hector said. Hector would not purchase it himself, but would let his order handle it for him. There were some 'official' arms dealers in the fraternity who could help him. They would laugh at him, for normally these guys sent shiploads of weapons to war zones, especially to the Middle East where it had been a source of unabated, sky-high profits for fifty years. In advance, he put up with the pitying looks of his fellow brothers.

In the last days in Soroca, Hector got to know the crew, but not the children, because they were not allowed to know about the action and had to react as spontaneously as possible. For them, it was a real vacation, although they did not find it very exciting to visit a wildlife park to see animals that surrounded them since childhood. They had been told that they would visit a wildlife park that was also an amusement park, but only the giraffes piqued their imagination.

Therefore, Hector met Milena, the animal tamer, who did not speak any foreign language. Malev translated all their communication, and as a result, Hector did not really get her opinion every time, but she did make a positive impression on him. The fact that she only spoke Moldavian, a sort of Romanian dialect, meant that if they were caught, an interpreter would be necessary, and it remained to be seen if they could find one and would be prepared to pay the costs. Hector saw it as an advantage. Nikita, a sister of Milena and the mother of Malev's niece, would be the driver. She spoke a mixture of languages, which made it possible for Hector to tell her directly what the intention was. The juggler, the young German, Heinrich, had set off into the wide world at the age of sixteen. After a lot of wandering, he ended up at Malev's circus, whom he now regarded as his family. He had broken with his own family and had virtually no contact with them. They did not know where he was and he wanted to keep it that way. Hector was delighted with him as well, especially since he was the only one of the main players who disposed of a foreign bank account. Malev had looked at Hector incredulously when he asked if the circus entrepreneur had a bank account. 'Why?' had been his reaction, and Hector could understand why. After all, it served no purpose in Malev's free life. The circus did have a bank account with a Moldavian bank, but the bookings of the flight to Cologne and the reservations at the car rental company were not to be traced back to the circus. Heinrich made the bookings and communication easier in German. Hector would transfer the costs in euros to him. As a precaution, he would do this from his son's company to protect himself as well as possible. Slowly but surely, the plan took shape and Hector felt in his own element. He thought the protagonists of the piece that would be performed, were great people who were not bothered with anything and saw the humorous side of it. The same went for Vladimir, the retired Russian sniper, who had served in his army for decades and now enjoyed his old age. He supplemented his meager pension by doing odd jobs for the circus. He also belonged to Malev's extended family.

'But,' Hector said when the whole company gathered in Malev's caravan, 'everything depends on that one moment that you get out until the moment you get back in. There must be as little time as possible between these two. This means that you do not wait until someone makes a video of it, but that you have already attracted the attention of a filming person. Only when you are one hundred percent sure that everything is being filmed, then it is high time for action.' That night, a lot of laughter and drinking of beer went on in Malev's damp caravan.

Chapter 12

Hector was a guest at the barbecue after the last performance. The circus had been allowed to stay in Soroca for two more days and Malev did not even have to pay anything extra for it. It was still early in the spring and the stream of tourists for the fort had not yet started. The past nine days they had been lucky with the weather, with an average of 21 degrees Celsius during the day and about five degrees lower in the evening. Moldova was known for its mild climate with a short, often harsh winter, and a long period over which the other seasons stretched. On average, the annual temperature was 17 degrees. Because the country was not next to the sea, it did not rain abundantly and during the circus performances, there had not been a raindrop.
Malev looked back on a successful week and the turnover had exceeded his expectations. The next day, the camp and the circus were broken down only to be rebuilt two months later, and then with the tent that they normally used for performances. The season had started well for Malev, and thanks to Hector's job, he did not have to worry at least for the rest of the year. Hector had explained to him that it had become enormously expensive to attract customers through advertisements due to the fragmentation of the media in Western Europe. That is why companies were increasingly looking for alternatives and their intended action was a good example of this. If it became a success, visitors would

come from far and wide to the wildlife park. No ad campaign could compete with that. Malev liked Hector and that feeling was mutual. They trusted each other and Malev had already apologized several times for the unorthodox way of their first meeting. The men clicked together and they spoke at a level where there was much hidden wisdom, or at least so they thought. The tickets were booked and everything for the trip was arranged. Malev had already received the first 15,000 euros from Hector in crisp notes of fifty euros. The wage per adult had been set by Malev at 1,500 euros, which was a fortune in Moldova. This way he got thirty-nine thousand euros for himself out of it. It made him happy and he hit Hector several times on his shoulders at the introduction round of the barbecue night. Because Hector was a friend of the big boss, he was immediately included in the group as one of them. After a festive evening with lots of meat and drink, the men said goodbye.

'Goodbye, and I'll see you in Reims,' Hector said when Malev embraced him, and Malev mumbled something in the same vein.

The next day, Hector flew back to Brussels. He looked back with satisfaction on his journey and on the good deal that he had made with Malev. Now it was up to him to arrange everything down to the last detail. At home, he made contact with the car mechanic who had long ago done repair jobs for Marc Dutroux when he was busy stealing cars. The mechanic switched the VIN of his stolen cars until it went wrong and Dutroux was put behind bars for three months. Meanwhile, girls died in his basement that had been left to their fate. At the criminal proceedings, Dutroux had insisted that he was part of a pedophile network, consisting of, among others, police officers, businessmen, bankers, doctors and high-ranking politicians. When it turned out that his criminal case would not focus on that, it sparked the anger of 300,000 people who spontaneously took to the streets in Brussels. It was called 'The White March' at the time. However, it did not have the desired result. Dutroux was the only one convicted for his crimes. The mechanic had a lucky escape and he considered Hector's assignment an easy job. Drilling two holes was a piece of cake. The restoration would take a little longer unless he replaced the entire tailgate, which was the best and the cheapest solution.

'It must be possible to open and close the holes, and a gun must be hidden in the car as well,' Hector said. He had given him the brand, color, and year of construction of the car in question.

That was no problem for the mechanic either, and Hector would accompany him to pick up the two cars at a hotel in Reims that would be parked in the neighborhood the next morning after their preparation. Hector wanted to prevent people from seeing that the license plates had been changed. They would do the same thing a day later, but then would restore everything back to its original state. For this, they would pick up cars at another hotel and bring them back in the neighborhood. Hector had worked out his plan well. That was also the case with the order and delivery of the weapon. As Hector had expected, his brothers had laughed about it, but he got what he needed anyway. He stored the box in which the Dan-inject double-barrel gun had been delivered at the mechanic's, and the false French license plates that had been produced elsewhere as well. Now he only had to wait for Malev and his crew.

Chapter 13

With an old seven person SUV, Malev, Vladimir, Milena, Nikita, Heinrich, and the two children departed to the airport in the capital Chisinau. They downloaded their tickets via the travel organization's website, and that was a good thing, because the postal delivery in Moldova was far from reliable.

'Once I have parked the car at the airport, we split up into three groups,' Malev said. 'I, Vladimir and Heinrich stay together and that also applies to Nikita and Valeria. Milena and Cosmo travel separately as well. In this way we prevent that we stand out as one group and we will be recognized later.'
For Valeria, Nikita's daughter, this was a sign that it would not be just a vacation. She looked at her mother questioningly.

'Does this mean we cannot sit next to each other in the plane?' she asked surprised, and the little Cosmo looked confused.
Malev answered that this was not allowed. Cosmo would have liked to sit next to Heinrich. He looked up to Heinrich a lot, and thought he was very cool. He saw him as a father figure, after his father had perished three years earlier in Transnistria, an elongated little dwarf state in the southeast, wedged in between Moldova and the Ukraine. Transnistria had declared itself an independent state, but it was governed by Moldova. It was on the other side of the Dniester River in the southwest of

Ukraine. The state wanted to become autonomous and be like a satellite state to the big Russia. It caused tensions in that region and Cosmo's father had been stationed there to maintain order. As a result of a stupid accident, he had died, to the intense grief of the son and his mother.

Milena was well aware that she played an important role in the company and she had decided to paint her blonde hair black in the hotel in Reims to prevent recognition. She was not nervous about it. She knew how to deal with cheetahs and from a leaflet that would be provided by the wildlife park, she got information about the times when the cheetahs were fed. After feeding time, the animals would not be dangerous at all and she did not worry about it. However, she had to be careful not to let anyone run, and certainly not little Cosmo because cheetahs were still wild animals that would react strongly to that. They could see her son as a prey. She had already figured out how it would develop, as Hector's film about the route and the place where it would to take place had been very useful for her. His drawings of the situation on the spot were also engraved in her memory. It reassured her that Vladimir would keep an eye on things, and could intervene with a rifle when it got out of hand. For Milena, it was only an insignificant action. Once it was over, they would have to leave the game park as quickly as possible.

'Just call me if you need help with anything,' Malev said to Nikita, while he held his mobile phone in the air.

Nikita and Valeria were the second couple to leave the SUV at the car park of the airport. Milena had already rushed ahead with Cosmo.

They did not give each other a glance while they were queuing in front of the check-in desk so their allocated seats were scattered through the plane. Cosmo had been given a coloring book, and he was coloring attentively and to his heart's content. He held his tongue between his lips in a corner of his mouth. Milena stroked her son's head fondly.

The direct flight to Cologne went smoothly and after two hours, they landed at Cologne-Bonn airport. When they had collected the suitcases, Nikita and Valeria were the first to go to the arrival hall after the customs check. It was agreed that Malev and Vladimir would get the cars from the rental company and that they would pick up Heinrich, the women and the children at the front of the main entrance of the airport.

Fifteen minutes later, Vladimir had already signed the papers and paid the deposit for the rental car in cash. Malev would not report to the rental counter before Vladimir had finished his formalities. The mobile phone rang in Malev's pocket, and he answered the call when he saw that it was from Nikita. He walked into the hall with the device on his ear.

'What is the matter?' He asked.

He could not understand Nikita because she spoke very fast and her voice sounded upset. After he had told her to calm down, she told the story understandably.

'A thousand times sorry, Malev,' she said. 'I am here with Valeria in the perfume shop and she has just been caught stealing a bottle of Chanel No 5. The manager wants to call in the airport police.'

Malev cursed and asked her where she was. He saw the store sign about a hundred yards away and sprinted towards it. Panting, he ran into the store where he saw Nikita and Valeria standing at the back desk in the building. The manager had a telephone in his hand. Wildly gesturing, he ran towards him. Malev evaluated that he had not yet had contact with the control room of the airport police.

'Sorry, sorry, sorry,' Malev said, slapping Valeria in the face. Immediately, tears welled in the eyes of the twelve-year-old. 'I'll be happy to pay for everything,' he said and asked how much the bottle cost. The manager, who was shocked by the slap that Malev had handed out, reported that the bottle cost 69 euros. Malev pulled out his wallet and took four 50-euro notes from it. 'Is this enough?' he asked. 'Sorry again, but we are in a hurry and I will have a heart-to-heart talk with the child later. Could you please let her go?'

The manager was in two minds about it and muttered something about protocols, which immediately stopped when Malev added another 50 euros.

'All right, but just for once,' he said, snatching the banknotes from the counter to the relief of Malev, who turned to Valeria and told her to put the bottle back on the shelf, which she did immediately. Malev shook the manager's hand and thanked him for his decision. He dragged Valeria out of the shop by her arm with great strides. Once in the hall, he was cursing at her and her mother, until he saw the frightened faces of bystanders and he snapped at Nikita to wait outside. He quickly walked back to the rental company where Vladimir was standing in front of the door with a car key, looking at him questioningly.

'Business as usual,' Malev whispered to him.

Chapter 14

Hector was visiting his son in Brussels. He returned the money in cash that Daan had transferred to a German bank account. He did not ask his father questions about it, because he thought it was not his business. He booked the transfer as a business transaction and put the money in his own pocket.

'And how is the crowdfunding going?' Hector asked. His son's beaming response was that the counter stood at four million euros and he thanked his father for his efforts.

'I do not know how you have managed it, but I am very happy about it. It looks good, and I am confident that we will get the rest of the amount as well,' he said. Together, they looked at the progress of the deposited money, which increased while they were looking at it. Many of the investors deposited a ton. Two even invested two and a half tons and there were remarkably many investors with several tens of thousands of euros. There were also participants with a hundred euros, which was the minimum amount. Hector explained it as the snowball effect. After all, if the big boys saw profits, it would be okay. The bycatch did not take any effort from Lex, and was the result of market forces. They talked about the plans with the company and Hector was proud of his enthusiastic son.

'How is your mother doing?' Hector asked him at lunch.

'Very well,' Daan, said 'she is totally into yoga and madly in love with her instructor, some sort of befuddled guru whom I do not trust, but she has to figure it all out for herself.'

Hector and his wife divorced six months ago, and although this had been a great relief for him, he had hardly spoken about it with anyone and he preferred to keep it to himself. Yet, he still felt closely involved with her. They had been through a lot together and he cherished his happy memories. Ultimately, the thrill had completely disappeared from their relationship and they lived together like brother and sister. The marriage had exceeded the expiration date. The fact that she was reinventing herself made him jealous, also that a psychedelic squatting king had his dirty paws all over his ex-wife.

'And, is it already a serious relationship?' Hector asked interestedly.

'Yes,' Daan said, 'they have been on holiday to India together.'

Hector decided to let the subject rest and thought it was high time that he also started looking for love again, but only when the job in the wildlife park had been brought to a good end.

Hector had asked the reception of the hotel in Reims to call him as soon as Malev had arrived. He did not have Malev's telephone number and he did not want it either, because this way his phone data would not end up on Malev's phone. Before reception would call him, they would check with the new guests first if they did not object. This was not the case when Hector was informed that evening of Malev's arrival. He jumped into his car and drove to the repair company of the mechanic, with whom he was going to pick up the cars. On the way, the mechanic said that he still needed one day and that he would not do the jobs the next night. For Hector, it was a small hitch, but it was no disadvantage, all things considered. It was Saturday and on Sunday, the wildlife park would attract many visitors because of the beautiful spring weather. On Monday, it was much safer for Malev and his crew and it reduced the chance of complications. Actually, he was glad to see the slight change of direction and his Moldavian friends had to make the best of it in Reims the next day.

The men entered the hotel and when Hector knocked briefly on the door with the room number that reception had given to him, Malev opened the door. The reunion was warm and Hector and Malev embraced each other as if they were brothers. Hector asked him for the spare key of one of the cars, and when he received it, he passed it on to the mechanic who was waiting for him at the beginning of the corridor. He already drove back with one car.

'Did you have a good journey?' Hector asked when he was back in Malev's hotel room.

'Yes, everything went perfect,' Malev replied.

Then Hector greeted Heinrich and Vladimir who als present. Hector asked how the women and children were, and they answered that they were doing well.

'I would like to greet them, is that okay?'

Malev agreed and took him into the hallway. He explained that Milena and Cosmo were on the same floor, and Nikita and Valeria were on the floor above. When Milena opened the door of her hotel room, she had a towel wrapped around her head and a trickle of black fluid seeped from under her turban. She let them in.

'What on earth are you doing?' Malev asked.

'Dyeing my hair,' Milena replied.

Malev sighed deeply and told her that it was not such a bad idea, but that she had blonde hair on her passport photo so she would have to change it back before they returned home. He wanted absolutely no hassle at the passport control. Malev translated it for Hector with a look of incredulity on his face. He rolled his eyes.

'Oh yes, of course, stupid, stupid, stupid,' she said, what Malev also translated for Hector in English.

She gave Hector a hand and unintentionally, a full look at her left breast because her dressing gown fell open and quickly closed it with her other hand. The little Cosmo stood beside her, clutching her left leg and looking curiously at the visitor.

Hector kneeled down and shook the boy's hand, the shy child endeared Hector with his beautiful eyes. Hector got

72

up and he wished Milena good luck, after which, the two men left the hotel room. Hector had stored the opened dressing gown in his memory and the erotic image had a special place between all the breasts that were worth saving. Hector asked with interest if Milena had a husband or boyfriend and Malev told him that her husband had unfortunately been killed. Again, Malev knocked on a hotel door and now Nikita was the one who opened it, also adorned with a towel around her head. She let the men into her room as well.

'Let me guess,' Malev said, 'you've dyed your hair.'

'Yes, I thought it was a good idea that Milena had. I now have blonde hair. Look,' she said, pulling a tuft from under her turban.

Malev looked at Hector and said that it was probably a virus. Nikita had also not considered that it could give problems with customs when they crossed borders. She said she would change it back after the visit to the wildlife park, although she thought it was bad for her hair. Her daughter was reading a comic book on a hotel chair. She had a black eye. Hector introduced himself to her and asked her how she got that eye. He did not get an answer until Malev told him that Valeria had run into a door. For Hector, the explanation was the one usually given for a child who had been beaten, just as it happened inside the fraternities. If you were a politician or another highly placed person, you could earn points if you appeared on the TV with a black eye. Hector had witnessed the ritual in his order where a brother got a black eye. It was seen as a great honor, just like this was the case in motor clubs – the ones that had not been forbidden - or student associations.

In a short time frame, Hector had received three signs of things he had not expected, and the same seemed to be the case with Malev. He was slightly worried about it, because apparently Malev did not control his people sufficiently in the interests of their assignment, for which they were richly rewarded. Back in Malev's hotel room, Hector made a comment about this. He approved that the women had died their hair, apparently on their own initiative, so it would be harder to recognize them. He emphasized 'apparently on their own initiative' and added that Valeria's face could not come into the picture because now she could be easier recognized precisely because of her black eye. Malev nodded that he understood his friend's message. Hector handed him the second envelope with 15,000 euros and said that the job had been moved to Monday. He explained to him where they could find the cars on Monday morning. On Wednesday morning, they would see him again at the other hotel, and that would be their last meeting for the time being. The cars would then also be returned to their original state. He would also give them back their spare keys. Everything had been arranged. Hector said his goodbye and added a 'Good luck'.

Chapter 15

Hector drove to the car mechanic with the other car and left his own car in the vicinity of the hotel. They would need it after driving up and down two times on Wednesday morning. Then he would have to use a loan car from the garage for transport. The whole operation required a lot of logistics, but Hector had thought everything out well. His hobby was playing chess and the analytical faculty of thought he had built up with this noble game now came in handy. It would have been easier if Malev and Nikita could pick up the cars at the mechanic's, but Hector did not want them to know who else was involved. Then they would never be able to make a statement about that. At the mechanic - who was waiting for him - he handed in the spare key of the second car and the mechanic looked at the rear window.

'They are rental cars,' he said. 'This means that the German license plates are engraved in all windows to prevent theft. These numbers will not match with the false French license plates, but it will have to do for one day. When I switch the VIN again, I have to transfer the rear window into the new tailgate. I've already taken it into account and ordered the new tailgate without a window.'

Hector had not thought about this, but the engravings were only visible up close. If they were caught, then the track would lead back to the German rental company, which was another reason for Hector that their action could not fail.

'This is where the holes have to be,' Hector said and he pointed to the place. The mechanic had to take into account the distance from the barrel of the gun to the visor and the viewing hole had to be larger than the hole for the barrel.

'Do you have a rental car for me?' Hector asked.

'Of course,' the mechanic replied, handing him a key to an unobtrusive old car used by his customers when their car was serviced or repaired.

The women and children stayed in their rooms in the hotel the next day, to prevent them from being recognized later. It was also a kind of revenge from Malev because the ladies had acted on their own. The three men made the night of it in Reims under the guise of a much-needed cultural journey of discovery through the old city that was founded by the Remi, a Celtic people, and dated from before the era. Then it was conquered by the Romans and they changed the town's name into Durocortorum. After the departure of the Romans, it became Reims. The current cathedral, dating from 1211, towered above the city and the location was where many French kings had been crowned in the past. Notre-Dame was a landmark for the men to walk toward although they were hampered by the many cafes along the way. They actually had no interest in the culture of the city, and in one establishment after another, they drank copious amounts of beer, until they switched to champagne, for which the town and the region were famous. They felt that their action had to be celebrated in advance. As time progressed, the men became increasingly noisier and they received admonishing glances from other cafe visitors. Malev was the only person who still had the presence of mind to blow off the pub-crawl and return to the hotel, where they slept off their intoxication in a siesta and went to bed early after a late dinner.

Hector had used the Sunday to check everything once more. The only thing he had no influence on was the moment supreme, on which the entire action centered. He would like to take control of it on the spot, but that was not possible and he just had to rely on Malev and his crew. That Sunday evening, he drove to the garage, where he determined that the mechanic had kept his word. The cars were equipped with French license plates and the holes had been drilled, which, as intended, could be almost invisibly closed. The anesthetic rifle was placed under the seat of the co-driver in such a way that it could not be seen from the outside. Through his mobile phone, Hector found the Moldavian translation of 'look under the seat of the co-driver' and he wrote it on a post-it that he stuck on the dashboard. That could be seen from the outside, but he considered it a negligible risk that the yellow note would be noticed by a casual passer-by who knew what it meant. As agreed, they parked the cars in the vicinity of the hotel, and for Hector, the rest was hit or miss.

Chapter 16

On December 1st, I started working for my new employer. I had finally found a job. This had been hard, because in Zeeland, where I live, there is not much employment to be found. Most jobs are in catering, but you have to have a talent for it and it is not really my thing. Out of necessity, I worked in several restaurants during the tourist season. There was not much else, apart from delivering mail, which I really enjoyed although it did not pay much. In the end, the stacks of brochures that had to be delivered together with the regular mail were too much for me, because of my bad back. It turned out I was not built to carry heavy bags around and the continuous getting on and off the scooter did not help either, especially when the weather was cold. I would have liked to continue delivering mail, but unfortunately, I could not and had to stop. I am sure the frightfully growling dogs that used to chase me every day, longing to put their shiny teeth into my calves, felt the same.

I had been a postman for six months, and the next year I was without a job. My father worked in West Brabant where the job offers were more varied. His job seemed interesting to me, and it would be nice if we could work together, but the employer did not have a suitable position for me until the day my father told me that his company was looking for recruits. Their need was great, because they could not find anyone. Although I did not have the required technical skills, this was a golden opportunity for me and I applied for the job.

'We have green light,' my father shouted a few weeks later as he burst into my room without knocking. I heard the enthusiasm in his voice. I had not counted on it anymore and was as excited as he was. Finally, I had found a job. It was about time, because I found the boredom of pointless sitting at home really taxing.

My first working day consisted mainly of tours across the departments alongside my father who introduced me to his colleagues. It was the day that I was also introduced to Henk and Joris. I wanted to get to know all the ins and outs of the company and look at every inch of the business premises. I am inquisitive and asked a lot of questions. I inquired about the function of everything that I did not immediately understand. During my lunch break, I met my colleague Henk in the canteen.

'I do not think it's normal that you have a long coat and I do not,' he said in a harsh tone.

I replied that was not my doing and knew nothing about it. In the days that followed, he continued to blame me in a more or less hidden way for having what he thought was a better coat. Even in my presence, he expressed his dissatisfaction with the supervisor in a way that made me feel personally attacked.

'Maybe it's because you are working here through an agency,' I tried.

'Maybe you are right,' he replied sullenly and walked away.

I had only just started working there and did not want any trouble with my colleagues. I took a different approach and tried to be as social as possible. His nagging about my coat aside, Henk could explain well, even better than my father, who knew everything, but often took something as self-explanatory, while the listener stared at him with glassy eyes. For me, it went into one ear and out through the other. I had little technical knowledge and did not understand some terms. Henk took the trouble to explain it to me in a simple way and I was grateful to him for that.

When I had worked at the company for two weeks, my alarm clock woke me up at four in the afternoon and I felt tired. I had not slept enough by far and the night shift had been hard work. I stumbled out of my bed and walked to the living room. Normally I saw my parents there, but that was not the case now. They had left a yellow post-it note for me on the round coffee table.

'Hi, your mother is not feeling well and we are now going to the doctor. We left at noon.'

It confirmed the frightened suspicions I already had. My mother had been feeling very ill for a while now and usually my parents planned a doctor's visit in the

afternoon, which corresponded with the time they
mentioned, but not with a regular visit, because she had
not told me about it. Thoughtfully, I stroked my chin
with my hand and decided to wait for them, because it
had been four hours since they left. I encouraged myself
that it would not be that bad and that they could return at
any moment, but it gnawed at me and I was startled when
the house phone rang. I rushed to the phone and grabbed
the handset firmly, as if it were a final straw that I wanted
to cling to. I heard my father's worried voice.

'Your mother is not doing well,' he said in an emotional
voice. 'She was admitted to the intensive care unit of the
hospital with extremely high blood pressure,' he
continued in a tone that was a bit firmer, but also
contained a sob as a harbinger of many emotions.
They had discovered high blood pressure, much too late
in my mother's life, which had caused a lot of damage in
her body and a permanent discomfort. A long period of
rehabilitation would be next for her.
After my father had finished his story, I quickly ate a
sandwich and hurried to the hospital. I felt as if in a daze,
as if all of this did not really happen. Dark and doom-like
scenarios haunted my head. As fast as I could, but in a
responsible manner, I drove to her. In the hospital, I ran
past the reception and saw the kiosk behind it. An
unwritten law for visiting a patient in a hospital dictates
that you should bring something of consolation or a
delicacy for the patient. I thought it was a strange rule

82

and not exactly my priority. Nonetheless, I felt I had to do something to cheer her up. After a quick glance through the little shop that smelled of lavender, I noticed the shelf with stuffed animals. Kittens and rabbits looked at me and I found one bunny that would suit my mother. The deep glow in the beady eyes of the fluffy little creature got to me. At the checkout, they asked me if it was a present for someone in the hospital, but it did not dawn on me. I was in shock and stammered something unintelligible from which they gathered the word 'mother'. The cashier wished her a swift recovery. I smiled, and was touched by her sympathy. I reported to the desk that I came to see my mother.

The receptionist told me where I could find her and she showed me the way. The corridors in the hospital made me dizzy and I felt anxious. In the corner of my eye, the walls and the ceilings turned something I blamed on my stress. I found her in the intensive care, in a web of connected wires, infusions, and medical devices.

Terrified, I looked at my father sitting next to the bed. He looked worried, but at the same time, tried to look as if everything was all right. I had five more steps to take and I did not know what to say for a moment. My only grip was the bunny that I held behind my back, which I produced without saying anything. There I stood with tears in my eyes and my mother spread her arms.

'Oh, that is so sweet,' she said, and she closed me in her arms.

Chapter 17

My training period at the company was not flawless, because my mother had ended up in the hospital. The result was that my father was often absent and I was more and more on my own. One day, when my father was not there, things went really wrong for the first time. I walked over to Joris, the manager, and asked him what I had to do that morning.

'You and Henk have to move some stuff. We are having an inspection tomorrow,' he said, giving me further instructions.

Henk, however, had other plans and he let me do the heavy work on my own. I understood well that as the youngest employee, I would get the rotten jobs, but this was a complete lack of solidarity. All this carrying heavy boxes was a disaster for my back and me. Yet, I fulfilled my task, as was expected of me. Henk had not come to help me, and when I had finished the job, I reported it to Joris.

'But where is Henk?' he asked, and he looked at me with a look of disbelief.

'I do not know that, sir,' I answered honestly and before Joris reacted, the door was opened with a bang.

'Where were you, goddamn it?' Henk yelled, bursting in and making wide gestures.

I was too shocked to give a reply or say anything. Full of disbelief, I listened to what he said about me. He claimed that he, not I had worked very hard. I was too surprised to say anything in my defense. Joris rebuked me for lying to him. Henk only received a warning because he had cursed, something Joris did not appreciate. After having broken my back for a day with those heavy boxes, my credits were taken away from me, and I even received the predicate to be a liar. Never before did I feel as betrayed as at that moment. I decided to do something about it and later, when I had calmed down, I returned to Joris. I told him the true story and I felt strong enough to file a formal complaint against Henk.

'Are you sure that's what you want?' Joris asked and he continued that this would not make me popular with management.

Later that afternoon, when I returned home, I asked my father what to do. He felt that it was indeed better to leave it as it was.

'This happens sometimes in the company,' he said. 'Henk has been employed four weeks longer than you, and in that month, he has already been in a fist fight with someone. If I had not intervened, they would have ended bashing each other. That, too, blew over without consequences for him, but I know that types like him never last long.'

I began to feel annoyed with my job and its cheerless environment, and in a short time, I had learned how things were settled on the shop floor, but I did not let them take advantage of me. I just did my best and hoped that the nagging and pestering would stop by itself. After

85

a few weeks without any positive changes, Henk was shouting in his mobile phone at his internet provider about his subscription. He was in Joris' office at the time. In the corridor, I met Joris and instead of confronting Henk, whose rant could be heard through the whole building, he turned and hurried back to the coffee machine.

'This is too crazy for me, I am really not going in there,' I could just hear him mutter. The man was clearly no match for Henk and although they often clashed, he had apparently given up the fight.

I thought of my father's words and hoped that Henk would quickly bugger off. I did not want to wait for that and I arranged a time-out to make a dream-trip, two months after my appointment. Since I was sixteen, I have had the ardent wish to go to Japan, the land of the rising sun, the blossoming trees and the Samurai. My parents helped me with the preparations. Everything had been arranged, but two days before my departure, my colleague, Mike, reported 'sick'. Joris instructed me in a compelling way to substitute for him. Two days before my departure, I had a lot to arrange, as it is for everyone who is making a long journey. I could not and would not comply with his order, because I would miss my plane and would have to go to Schiphol Airport straight after work with the stress still bottled up inside. Mike reported sick more often and I had the strong suspicion that he was sometimes faking, but of course, I could not prove that. Absenteeism was high at the company and I had already taken over many services from 'sick' colleagues. All the time, they appealed to me to substitute for colleagues on holiday. I had always agreed to be on the right side, but now it was my turn and I refused to take over the shift.

At Schiphol, I walked with my parents to the exchange office where I exchanged my euros for yen. Japan has a society based on cash and it is hard to find an ATM machine or pay with a card. Fortunately, I knew this beforehand. Just before I went through customs, my mother hugged me. She would never make such a trip herself, because she had a great fear of flying. Emotionally, we said goodbye to each other. On board the plane, I let it go and I could relax after all the hassle that comes with arranging a flight. I did not have a fear of flying, but I hated all that fuss and bother. I was sitting next to two friendly men who turned out to be colleagues. I sat between them and asked them if they wanted to sit next to each other. I was prepared to switch seats with one of them.

'No, no, I am happy that I do not have to sit next to him. We see each other enough at work,' the eldest of the two said. It was a pleasant flight and we talked a lot. They were on a business trip to Dubai.

'I have to go a bit further,' I said laughing, the way I usually speak. Much of what I say comes out laughing. I do not know from which side of the family I got this, but it is just something in my genes. They were impressed by the fact that I was traveling to Japan, and they wanted to visit the country one day. The flight was long and the time could not be filled with just pleasant conversations, so we decided to watch a film in the head restraints of the chairs in front of us. I chose Indiana Jones, the man who visited distant places and was the discoverer of special artifacts. I thought that was appropriate for my first trip alone, although it was in fact a group trip, of which I had not yet met the other participants. The huge two-story airbus beamed through the atmosphere towards the rising sun.

The men who had sat next to me wished me a prosperous trip. I had a stopover in Dubai. At the airport, where I would stay for four hours, I met a fellow traveler from my group trip. It was a middle-aged woman and we immediately had pleasant conversations at the gate. At the boarding, it turned out we did not have seats close to each other. Again, I was sitting in between a couple. This time I was in between a Japanese elderly couple. Their English was flawed and there were pauses, but I still learned a lot about Japan. As support for this, I got a list of Japanese expressions that my mother had compiled for me. The woman laughed at my stammering pronunciation, but she appreciated it very much that I tried.

After a total journey of eighteen hours, I landed in Osaka, the third largest city in the country with 2.7 million inhabitants. We would visit Tokyo, the capital, as well. I had read a lot about it and had got a dislike of Tokyo. I did not look forward to visiting it that much. I was much more interested in Osaka, because it had more history. I got to know the entire group and we visited the mountain town of Magome. It was built up vertically and very special. Along the steep main street, gutters drained the water off the mountain. The shops had all kinds of stuff, such as wooden kendo swords that would never fit in my suitcase. Instead, I bought a Katana keychain, which I still cherish.

Our travel guide was very interested when I told him enthusiastically about my YouTube channel.

'Maybe, one day, I'm going to be famous,' he said.

Chapter 18

When I was younger, my friends, Niels, Lucas, and I
were enthusiastic about making films and I dedicated a
lot of time to it. We made reviews about various
activities in Zeeland such as; carting, pooling, laser
gaming, or simply a walk through the historically
beautiful and interesting Zierikzee. Although I was
originally not from Zeeland, I wanted to promote my
province. We filmed for our small target group of friends
and family. In the course of time, Lucas dropped out
because he had to cover such a long distance every time,
so just Niels and I remained. When my camera fell on the
ground and broke, my dream was also shattered. I gave
up, because I had already spent a lot of money on this
adventure. Because we did not share any other hobbies,
the contacts with Niels became far and few between. His
life changed and the friendship we once had vanished.

In the time that we often visited each other, Niels showed
me a leaflet: extras were needed for a movie about the
Zealandic naval hero Michiel de Ruyter. Part of it would
be filmed in Zierikzee. We signed up and were extremely
enthusiastic when we were invited. In an e-mail with an
explanation of the roles they had in store for us, they
wrote that I was allowed to figure in three scenes. They
had a robbery in mind for me. Also a role as a helper in a
warehouse and as a participant in a lunch party in front of
the house of the glorious naval hero. Niels was only

chosen to act as a filler. He was disappointed, because he would have liked to play in my scenes as well. I felt bad for him and suggested that he send an e-mail to the production company. To our surprise and to the delight of Niels, his request was honored. We were allowed to play together in the scenes and would turn it into a contest who would be pictured best in the movie.

On the day of the shooting, I picked up Niels at his home in Zierikzee, and on foot, we went to the designated assembly point. We were delighted and looking forward to it. It fit in our dream of everything that had to do with the world of film and video.

After a long walk, we arrived at a shed on a deserted terrain. It turned out to be one of those prefab units that had been filled to the brim with attributes for the seventeenth-century extras. The people who had been invited flocked on the premises and we had nice conversations with our new colleagues, who sometimes came from far away. We spoke to people who had traveled all the way from Groningen to Zierikzee. Behind the unit, the registration started and we had to sign a contract that prohibited us from mentioning anything about this day on the social media.

Niels and I were referred to the costume department, where a personal dresser dressed me. Then I had to go to the make-up where they put black sweeps on my face to make me look like a poor bloke from the golden age. The catering was well taken care of at lunchtime, but because of the nice conversations we had with our now nicely dressed fellow characters, I forgot to eat something.

After lunch, I saw Frank Lammers, the main actor, who was then at the make-up department. I waved excessively to him, and he nodded friendly.

Finally, we were picked up by a white van and driven to the first set. It was an old barn, which was still far from suitable to serve as a decor. Our fellow players and the two of us were asked to help to clear the barn. We got a lot of junk out of the abandoned building. When the job was done, which we had all done together, one of the production people came to me.

'Do you want to roll a beer barrel for the film?' he asked. 'The barrel is empty and not heavy, but you have to pretend it's a heavy load.'

It involved large wooden barrels of a well-known beer brand, which despite the promise, were quite heavy, so I did not have to act. After five takes, I was already pretty tired and that was just the beginning, because it always turned out that, the main characters had not been filmed perfect enough. It had to be re-shot 31 (!) times in total until I was released from my heavy duty.

Niels, who had an easier role in this scene, walked towards me.

'Piece of cake, right!' he said.

I looked at him sideways and we both laughed. He had watched my endless lugging from close by and he knew that I had had a hard time.

We had to move on to the next set in the center of Zierikzee and my stomach growled.

'If only I had eaten something,' I said, and I could beat myself for not eating anything at lunchtime when I had the chance. Niels confessed that he had not eaten anything either, because he had also been too busy with other things.

In Zierikzee, we had to take part in a chaotic scene in an angry crowd, who plundered a supply cart. I was ordered to steal a bag of food and run away with it, but the actors on the cart played so realistically that I found this very hard to do. It did not suit my character and I could not imagine it sufficiently, which made me dissatisfied with my input. During the many waiting times, I found out that Zierikzee was supposed to be Amsterdam in the movie. Amsterdam itself was not suitable because there are no such large-scale historically correct areas anymore.

After this scene, our growling stomachs had grown into real hunger. Niels did not suffer as much from it. He was also in better shape. I went to the catering shed, with hurting feet from the ill-fitting clogs I was wearing. I asked for a sandwich and got one that belonged in the era of the movie: stale and not suitable for consumption, but a snack from the candy bar fortunately satisfied my hunger at last.

They were also filming in the evening, and it was very chilly. The shirt that I was wearing under the open jacket was way too light, and I was feeling cold. They did not have anything warmer, so I decided to wear my own sweater under the shirt. That was not allowed because it did not match the seventeenth century, but for me, necessity knows no law.

'Can you see my collar?' I asked Niels after changing clothes.

'Yes, a little,' he replied.
I looked for something to cover the collar of my turtleneck and found a crate of scarves in the shack.

'Do you think you should do that,' Niels said, betraying that he disagreed with it.

'No one wanted to help me,' I replied. 'I'll put it back, honestly, when we hand in our costumes.'
With a scarf around my neck, we walked back to the set for the last scene, the lynching.
A fellow extra, who knew about my hunger, threw me an apple from one of the baskets that was intended for the crew. I was grateful and practically ate the fruit completely with the core. Since lunchtime, the catering had been badly organized and once again, I stopped my hunger a bit.
At the house of Michiel de Ruyter, we felt connected to the set of that time. Now I could imagine the role better.

'We lynch that traitor!' I cried heroically to my fellow characters, while the cameras were not even running yet.
I thought I was being tough, but those awfully pinching clogs were still bothering me a lot. It caused a grimace on

my face, but that fit in well with my role. Niels and I had a good feeling about our approaching acting violence. At four o'clock in the morning, we went wild.

When Anna de Ruyter addressed the crowd, we were allowed to determine for ourselves whether we agreed with her. I decided to choose her side. After her speech, the crowd became restless and we acted as if we were fighting each other without going too far, because that was only reserved for the professionals.

Most people, including young children, had become tired and irritated. The director also suffered from this and was no longer that easy going at this time at night, and he wanted to finish the very last scene as quickly as possible. This scene depicted the funeral of Michiel de Ruyter; his lifeless body sailed on a boat through the gates of Zierikzee. When that was on film, people cheered. Not because of his death, but because it was finished and we could hand in our clothes.

Niels and I said goodbye in front of his house and I drove home. At home, my mother was waiting for me on the couch. She was very curious and wanted to know how it went. I told her extensively during a hearty breakfast. The black soot was still on my face.

A year later, the film was released and I went to the cinema premiere with Niels and my parents. It turned out that I was more visible in the movie than Niels.

A few years later, I wanted to reunite the group of friends. I thought it was a shame that it had fallen apart. I suggested that we set up a YouTube-channel. The intention was that we would become well known by making videos of our personal experiences, as some successful vloggers had done before us. I called the channel 'First Person Everything' and I bought a headcam and a program to edit videos. Unfortunately, we did not get many followers, even though it was our intention to become famous with it, or at least famous enough to make some money with it. It did not become a success, however, despite our many attempts. I decided to change direction with a new concept, which in my eyes could not possibly fail, namely humor, and we changed the name of the channel into 'FPE humor'. No one knew what the name stood for, except for the people who had watched our older vlogs. It also gave us the opportunity to offer a broader range with humor as the common denominator. It was a good chance for us to develop our skills. Niels became a better speaker, and Lucas' stage fright quickly disappeared. I focused on the technical side and did the promotion, subtitling, editing, and in fact, the total production. Initially, my mother was skeptical about it, but gradually she also started to see the fun of it and helped us in many ways, she undertook make-up, costumes and catering to name a few things. What we did not own already was rented or purchased by my parents and the sketches were getting better. We received nice reactions, but again, we did not break through, which I had set as a personal goal. I did everything for it and much more than my friends, who only reported themselves on the days that we filmed.

As often under these circumstances, there was resentment about the difference in effort in relation to the future yield, which was still a distant dot on the horizon. While Lucas was already spending the money we had not made yet, Niels and I had a completely different vision of what we would do with the profits. We thought it was important to invest it in order to make our videos even better. 'You've got to spend money, to make money,' was my motto, and Niels agreed. We quarreled a lot and then made up again, but it was no longer fun. To get the joy back, I decided to let go of my target and to do it for the honor, as a hobby that had gone too far. This way, I did not need to chase Niels and Lucas to get moving to do a simple job such as promoting our channel. The same applied to the commitments they did not keep. Slowly, it all fell apart and I decided only to upload my own videos, like my trip to Japan. We kept in touch with each other, but little was left of the dream we once shared.

Chapter 19

My trip to Japan had been good for me and I was feeling
myself again. I could take on the entire world, and I was
doing well despite the frequent trouble with Joris and
Henk. I tried to deal as little as possible with Henk by
swapping shifts, so we were not rostered in to work
together. That was not very heroic, but I was tired of the
constant confrontations with Henk. After an early shift, I
came home tired in the afternoon.

'I have a surprise for you,' my mother said.

'A surprise? I'm curious,' I said.

She had bought tickets for the wildlife park that I always
loved to visit when I was a child. We had not been there
for years, and I thought it was a nice surprise.

'Can I drive, as you promised me?'

'Yes, I keep my promise,' she said and laughed.

So she had not forgotten that it was a childhood dream of
mine to drive the car in the wildlife park. I obtained my
driver's license when I was eighteen, now six years ago.
The cold months passed and gradually the weather
became better. In the meantime, Henk had received five
complaints, but to my surprise, he had not lost his job.
Spring was approaching, and my mother was still in the
process of recovering. She had difficulty walking and
therefore the visit to the wildlife park would be perfect
for her, because after a few steps she was already tired.
My father and I were working different shifts all the time,
so we hardly ever had our time off on the same days. It

turned out it was not that easy to find the right day for
our trip, but in the end, we planned it on Monday, May
7th. An additional advantage was that it would probably
not be very busy in the wildlife park.

'Did you get the cans?' my mother asked my father that
morning.
She looked pale and she was not feeling very well. She
would rather stay at home, but I persuaded her with the
argument that it would not be strenuous for her.
We drove to the wildlife park by car, with cans and
sandwiches in the cooler. During the ride, my father and I
talked about the idiot Henk, and Joris' very weak attitude.
When we entered the wildlife park, I immediately
recognized the large welcome signs. It reminded me of
the past. It brought back the memories of my youth and
the excitement of getting close to wild animals.
We joined in the queue and received the tickets from a
park officer. I put my hand on my father's shoulder.

'I could drive, remember?' I said laughing.
We swapped places and the park officer wished us a
pleasant stay. At walking pace, we entered the area of the
African wild dogs, but there was no dog to be seen. Until
my father saw the group that had hidden behind trees,
they used the brown leaves that were still on the trees as
a camouflage. After we had watched them extensively for
a while, I drove on and approached the part of the park
with the cheetahs, which was indicated by signs on the
right and left hand side of the road. There was a line of

cars in the direction of the cheetah area and I joined the queue in the back. We moved slowly in procession and after about ten minutes, we saw the cheetahs lying lazily in the shade of the trees on our left. They looked relaxed, and one of them seemed to be in a deep sleep. Two others seemed to be purring and occasionally showed their belly when rolling through the grass.

'They do have a good life here,' I said to my mother.She agreed and said she would like such a life for herself. There was a serene calm in the car, and among the cheetahs. There were no other cars behind us so I had the time to take pictures with my smartphone. The lazing animals reacted alertly to a passing car from the park. Only then, we saw that one cheetah was isolated in a cage further away, hidden among the trees.

'That's probably a male,' my mother said.
The cheetahs looked interested at the pick-up of the park and I wondered aloud whether it was feeding time. My father took the flyer from the park.

'What a pity,' he said after studying it, 'we just missed the feeding time.'
My mother and I also regretted it.
Now there was calm among the cheetahs, as they had resumed their afternoon nap. I took more photos with my phone.

'Shall I open my window a little to make better shots?' I asked.
Immediately, my mother panicked slightly.

'Have you gone crazy? Do you have any idea how fast these animals can be?'
Of course, I understood that she was absolutely right.

'Not even a little bit?' I asked, only to tease her, but she did not understand that and absolutely did not want to hear any more about it.

'They are even lying next to the car,' she said to me with indignation in her voice while she pointed in their direction.

'Why do you think we have to keep the windows closed in the park,' she said, shaking her head in disbelief.

'Yeah, yeah, I understand,' I said, 'it was just a joke.'
I started filming the cheetahs and in the corner of my eye, I saw a car in the right-hand mirror that did not queue behind us.

'French license plate,' my father said when they passed us. The French parked somewhat diagonally about twenty meters away from us and to my surprise, I saw the driver's door was opened and the right door as well.
A woman with dark mid-length hair got out, while the blonde-haired driver put her left leg outside the car on the ground while she remained seated. The woman on the right took a rucksack and something else that I could not see properly out of the car. Then she walked leisurely to the back of the car, where she opened the tailgate and stored her things. Meanwhile, a child of about four years old and even a young man who took pictures of the cheetah got out of the car as well. While all this

happened, a car with a Dutch license plate parked next to them.

In utter amazement, my mother and I looked at each other and only at that moment was when I realized that I caught all of it on film. Clearly visible, I aimed my mobile at them and I shouted that I was filming this. I could hardly believe what was happening in front of us and I was overwhelmed by disbelief. For a moment, I shifted my focus to the three cheetahs in the grass and I saw that they were raising their heads and showing interest in the developments surrounding the French car. It led to one of the cheetahs growling and baring her teeth, after which the driver quickly closed her door. The child was already back in the car while the woman and the young man were still outside, but now they also rushed back to the safety of the car.

When my mother saw the little child, she let out a cry of fear. She waved wildly with her arms to catch their attention, and then tapped her right finger on her right temple to make it clear that they were not right in the head. I, too, made such gestures, but it appeared they did not see us, although it was clear that they were looking in our direction. I wanted to honk my horn, but decided not to do so because it might have scared the cheetahs and who knows, those idiots might not have survived. During the whole incident, I hardly dared to breathe. When they were back in their car, I heaved a deep sigh of relief.

Fortunately, the cheetahs had stayed in their place and not moved towards them.

It took a while before we spoke to each other, because we were so very confused. We could hardly believe what we had just seen. The French car drove off and when we had somewhat recovered from the shock, I saw that the cheetahs were getting up one by one. I did not know why they did this, and decided to continue our tour. Farther along, we saw the same French car on the road at the bottom of a hill near a tree. I looked in amazement when I saw that the French family, with the little boy in their midst, were casually walking on the hill. They looked around as if they were looking for a suitable place to picnic. For the second time that day, I could not believe my eyes. The cheetahs bolted in front of our car and took on the posture that they use when they stalk a prey. Routinely, they prepared for their group-wise attack. I could see what their target was. They were after the child. The cheetahs started to run and I accelerated and raced around the corner.

'Not so fast!' my mother yelled, to which I reacted by reducing the speed while I remained focused on the slope and the people walking around there. The cheetahs dashed on the hill and I stopped the car. The five French people apparently realized that it was a dangerous undertaking to leave the car and one after the other swiftly returned to their car. We saw a cheetah hissing in an aggressive stance, while a girl of about thirteen, who we had not seen before, walked in front of the car and went into the car behind the young man. The dark-haired woman had taken the child on her arm. Strikingly quiet, and convincingly untroubled, she walked back to the car with the child. She continued to look at the cheetahs while warding them off with hand gestures. She showed no fear, but she had to be very aware that she had to get herself and the child to safety as quickly as possible. She was the last one to close the door behind her.

In the short time it had taken, we could do nothing to help. I recorded it on film but I was not even aware of that. We were there, we saw it, and we shrieked with horror. We were in shock, my hands were trembling and in a reflex, I had filmed everything with my smartphone that rested in my hands and on the steering wheel. My mother's hands were clenched into fists, something I had seen earlier when she was watching a horror film. She opened her hands and I saw that the imprint of her nails were etched in her palms. It had hurt her and she remedied it by rubbing her palms against each other. Speechless and upset, we stared ahead of us.

Out of nowhere, two jeeps of the park came at full speed from the opposite direction.

'Look! Help is on its way,' my mother cried, 'there are probably cameras around here and someone saw it or it is reported by someone!'

To our surprise, the jeeps drove past us at full speed, giving the French the opportunity to drive off and disappear from view.

'Shouldn't we go after them?' my mother said.

'And then what?' my father asked. 'We will never catch up with them anyway.'

I drove on and we left the cheetah territory, all the time peering between the trees to catch a glimpse of the French, but they were no longer to be seen. We no longer paid attention to the wildlife and dazed, we followed the road to a sandy parking lot, where we searched for the car again, but did not find it. My father suggested a break, and I was glad that I could stretch my cramped legs as the tension seemed to have been transferred there. My mother was still looking around the parking lot in the hope of discovering the French, and then we walked towards a building with toilets. I felt like a zombie who was no longer able to think normally, the incident had such a big impact on me. We walked past a souvenir shop.

'Shall we buy something to console us?' my mother suggested who knows me through and through and knows that I was very upset with the incident and could not get it out of my mind.

'All right,' I answered her monotonously, and I followed her inside.

The shop was full of toy animals from large to small and made from all kinds of materials. My mother pointed to a sculpture of a cheetah that looked realistic. She picked it up carefully.

'What do you think of it?' she asked, 'should I buy it?'

'All right,' I replied for the second time.

'It's for the sideboard in the living room,' she said, 'as a positive reminder of this day instead of the shock we had today.'

I understood very well what she was trying to do, but it did not take away my feeling of unease. Such a statue would not change anything, perhaps the opposite, however sweet she meant it.

There was a queue at the checkout and we shuffled past the bins with stuffed toys. She looked for a plush cheetah and pressed it into my hands.

'We buy this as well,' she said resolutely. 'After all, your bunny also helped me in the hospital.'

This was too much for me and I handed it back to her.

'I gave you the bunny when you were ill, but I am not ill and I am not a child anymore, ' I said and I went outside. My mother followed me; she had not bought anything.

Our fun day out had been ruined completely, but we still had to continue the route through the park. The Highland cattle, elephants, giraffes, and ostriches did not manage to draw our attention and on autopilot, I drove out of the wildlife park. We wanted to report the incident, but there was no one from the park at the exit. After payment, we pulled a coin from a vending machine to get out of the park and we helped a foreign couple who understood nothing of the vending machine. The sun was burning fiercely on my skin. I got two cans of soda from the car, gave one to my mother and stood in the shade next to her.

'Come on, we'll walk back into the park to report it,' my mother said impatiently and irritably. A bit farther, I saw wheelchairs under a roof.

'Shall I get you a wheelchair?' I asked.

'No, leave it,' she said, 'I will manage.'
The expression on her face revealed that she was in pain and that she did not want to admit it.
At the entrance, which was near the exit, a young employee from the park checked out tickets. We handed her our tickets and we walked through to look for a staff member to whom we could report the incident. This part of the park was deserted and we did not find anyone. After walking around in the heat for a while, my mother could not go on any further. We gave up and walked back.

'I'll send them an e-mail when we get home,' she said. Silently and with a heavy heart, I drove home. Each of us tried to process the incident. The day that seemed so much fun to us in advance had resulted in a dramatic fiasco.

Chapter 20

Malev programmed the navigator in Nikita's car.

'We are leaving now and you will set off in ten minutes. I do not want us to drive close to each other on the way,' he said.

Nikita understood and nodded her head.

'But what do we do once we are at the park?' she wanted to know.

'Inside the park, I also drive ahead and choose a spot with a good view of the tree that you saw in Hector's instruction video. You will recognize it when you see it. Heinrich will wait for you at the entrance gate and get into the car with you. We will keep in touch via the mobile phone,' he said, and he turned around.

Ten minutes later, Nikita reported to Malev that they were leaving. The journey took three and a half hours, something Milena had not counted on. It took her by surprise.

'That's quite a long way,' she sighed, 'and twice in one day. We have to stop once on the way, otherwise, it will be too long for Cosmo.'

She looked behind her and saw that her son was playing a game on his tablet. She warned him that he could become nauseous if he kept looking down all the time and said that there were also nice things to see outside. The child was immersed in his game so he did not respond to her. Valeria knew that she was in danger of becoming carsick and she stared at the town they passed, and a bit later, at the landscape. She was still furious that Malev had given her a black eye and that her mother had not prevented it, regardless of the reason for it. She thought it had been an exaggerated reaction and a far from corrective measure by someone who broke every rule himself and had done everything in his life that God had forbidden. She still felt the blow in her face, even though she had taken paracetamol for it. She felt there was a tense atmosphere. She had no idea why, but she knew it had something to do with the wildlife park. She did not really care and trusted that she would be back in Moldova in a few days. She was madly in love and wanted to go back to her boyfriend. She hoped that her black eye would have cleared by then; otherwise, she would use make-up to mask it.

After about two hours, they stopped at a roadside restaurant and as if her aunt had read her thoughts, she handed her a jar of make-up.

'Here hon, use this to mask your black eye,' she said.
Valeria took the offered jar.

'Why have you two dyed your hair?'
Before Milena responded, she looked around to check if someone was listening to their conversation.

'So we are not recognized,' she whispered.
Valeria did not understand this at all, but she did not care either, and she leaned forward in front of a mirror to put the make-up on her injured eye.

'There is Heinrich on the right side of the road,' Nikita said when they were about hundred yards from the park entrance. 'Will you make room for him?' she asked the two children in the back seat, but Milena wanted Cosmo to sit on her lap. While they were queuing for the ticket booth, Nikita phoned Malev. They had spoken three times on the way via their mobile phones. She knew that he and Vladimir were already at the park and that they had a good journey.

'We are now standing near the cheetahs,' Malev said, 'they've just been fed and are now quietly lounging under the trees. Several cars are parked here. We are now continuing towards the tree. Good luck.'
Nikita clutched her steering wheel; her knuckles turned white.

'Relax,' Milena said, putting her hand on her sister's arm.

'Everything will be all right,' she said.
Then she made it clear to everyone in the car that she was in charge and that they had to do exactly what she said. Even if it did not sound logical, they had to follow her instructions very carefully and without any form of protest. Then nothing bad would happen and they would soon be back on the way home. She gave them all one by one a penetrating look and asked if they all understood her. One after the other confirmed that they clearly understood the message.

'All right then, here we go,' she said as she drove into the park.

Quiet, but faster than most cars, Nikita drove through to the area of the cheetahs, where she saw a grey car.

'The cheetahs should be in the grass near the grey car on the left,' she said.

'Look out for people who are filming from their car. If you see people filming, you must tell me immediately,' Milena said.

'Yes,' Heinrich said while they were driving past. 'The driver of that car is filming the cheetahs in the grass.'

Milena had already noticed this as well and she instructed Nikita to park the car a little farther.

'And now what?' Nikita asked when the car had come to a standstill.

'Open your door and turn your body outside halfway. Then put your feet on the ground and keep an eye on the animals and the people in that car. When the animals come towards you, you close your door as soon as possible.'

She also opened her door and picked up her rucksack, which was at her feet, and the pillow she had sat on during the journey. Without losing sight of the cheetahs, she walked to the tailgate and just before she opened it, she called her son.

'Come outside, Cosmo,' she said, 'BUT NO RUNNING and stay very close to me.'

'Yes, Mom,' the little one replied.

'Heinrich, now you get out of the car with your camera and stand next to me. The cheetahs are still safely in place. Concentrate on the people in that car.'
Heinrich got out and held an antique photo camera in front of his face. In the meantime, he reported to Milena.

'They are making wild gestures,' he said, 'and they are tapping their fingers against their heads, like we are crazy.'

'Good,' Milena said, 'but are they filming us?'

'The driver has his mobile phone directed at us, so I assume he is filming.'
One of the cheetahs hissed at them and showed her teeth, which was a sign for Nikita to close her door and the three stepped back into the car. Valeria had stayed in the car all this time.

'We have a catch!' Nikita reported to Malev and she briefly told him what had happened. She also described the car and gave him the Dutch license plate number.

'Well done,' Malev said. 'We can see you driving towards us, but where is that grey car?'
Nikita looked into her rear-view mirror and saw that she was not being followed. Malev feared that the incident had been reported. If the park rangers came to the spot, everything would have been for nothing and they did not yet have enough footage. He thought quickly.

'Everyone get out! Now!' he screamed through his phone. It sounded so loud that everyone in the car heard it. Milena got out and took Cosmo on her arm.

112

'Walk up the hill now, but not too far,' she said to the other three who had also got out. There was no cheetah to be seen, but she knew that they would soon become active if they thought they could catch something. She saw that the grey car was at a distance of about 30 meters and that the driver was filming everything.

'Here they are!' Nikita shouted when she saw three predators coming towards her at a rapid pace.

'Wait!' Milena cried. 'Wait for my sign!'
She had to make her sign sooner than she had expected and she was amazed at the speed of the cheetahs, she was not used to this from her animals in the cage of the circus.

'DO NOT RUN!' she screamed.
Despite her warning, she could not prevent Nikita, Heinrich, and Valeria from rushing back to the car with a bit too much speed. She also walked at a brisk pace and kept the legs of Cosmo as high as possible. She was the last one to reach the car and hurriedly opened the door, sat down, and closed her door with a bang.

'Okay, now let's get out of here,' she said to Nikita. Her heart skipped a beat when two pick-ups from the wildlife park approached them from the opposite direction and in high speed. She was relieved that they drove past.

'They're searching, but they don't know what they're looking for and thank God, they're heading in the wrong direction,' Malev said on the phone and told Nikita to

113

leave the park as quickly as possible, without driving remarkably fast.

'I give you cover by following you, but once again, calmly, but as fast as possible.'

Chapter 21

The day out, which should have cheered us up,
completely turned our world upside down. At home, my
father went into the kitchen to prepare dinner, as he had
done every day in recent months since my mother was
discharged from the hospital. She was very tired from the
hectic day and she stumbled to bed after dinner.

'I'll send that e-mail to the park tomorrow,' she said.
I retired to my room and looked at the films I had made
that day. Filled with disbelief, I stared at the images
repeatedly and relived what had happened. Just like in
the afternoon, I was shocked and felt uncomfortable. I
wanted to share this feeling with my friends and
acquaintances. Editing had sort of become my second
nature, so it was not very difficult for me. I doubted
whether I should put everything on my YouTube
channel, and decided only to show the second trip.
The reactions came immediately and they were varied in
nature. I did not defend myself in an answer and I
gathered from it that not everyone understood the
situation in which we had ended up. I wanted to clear up
any misunderstandings and the next day, I stuck the film
of the first time the French family got out of the car in
front of it. This made it clear for everyone what had
happened. The reactions had one thing in common;
almost everyone was as astonished as I was. No one
thought this was normal behavior in a wildlife park. Niels
was one of the few who was less impressed. According to

him, the family had not been in danger. His comments disappointed me because he ignored that it had such a profound impact on us. It also made me angry; I thought he was not very understanding and was too matter-of-fact about it. I had not expected this from him, a more understanding attitude would have been appropriate. Lucas' comment was, 'They are one sandwich short of a picnic. The entire family must be retarded!' He also did not see how emotional this had been for us.

Our family was still upset for days after the incident. It kept us in its grip and not much remained of our daily routine. From the first night, my mother suffered from nightmares in which she experienced the attack of the cheetahs over and over again. It also affected her appetite to the point that she did not eat anything of the food her husband prepared for her.

I sometimes saw a cheetah in the corner of my eye, when I looked into the garden. The high grass and the dry brown spots in the hedge made it look like they were really sneaking around. It gave me chills and when I had these visions more often, I grabbed the lawnmower from the shed and put a stop to the high grass and my worries. It worked, because afterwards, I did not see them anymore.

We had planned our removal but everything still had to be packed. We moved to West Brabant because it was closer to our work. The long daily commute was getting to us.

After another night of packing, we decided that we had done enough for that day. We collapsed on the couch. It was around twelve and the TV was on. I was not paying attention, but softly heard something about cheetahs and to our amazement, we saw in a short flash the images I had put on YouTube on the late news. We were speechless. The sound was far too soft to be able to hear it properly and none of us could find the remote control, so we missed the comment from the newsreader. In tension, we waited for the repeat.

'It's beginning,' I announced superfluously when the opening tune of the news sounded.

The incident with the cheetahs was announced in advance and a little later, I saw my video on the entire screen.

'Where did they get that?' I wondered and continued that the last time I checked I only had 156 views. Now I checked again and to my surprise, I saw that it had been viewed 150,000 times. I thought it was a mistake of YouTube, which I had seen before when the number of viewers had been corrected the next day. In the meantime, it had become 2 o'clock and my need for sleep was winning from the adrenaline that I had built up. My father had already gone to bed and I wanted to follow his example, but my mother wanted to see one more repeat of the news. She was so impressed that she could not sleep that night. After the umpteenth attempt to fall asleep, she gave up. The persistent irritating rattle of incoming e-mails on the computer in the living room was not beneficial for a good sleep either.

'Wake up!' I heard in the distance, while it felt that I had only just fallen asleep. I turned around and imagined that I had dreamed it.
It was still dark outside.

'Come on, you have to wake up,' my mother said to me and she patted my arm. 'I cannot keep them off any longer.'

'Keep them off?' I asked surprised. 'What are you talking about? What time is it?'

'Half past four,' she said.
Half past four! I thought, what the hell am I supposed to do at half past four in the morning?
I was free that day and had no appointments.
My mother had been up all night answering e-mails, and she felt that it would be better if I answered some of them myself. Even more because they explicitly requested this. It did not get through to me, and I told her it could wait a little longer. There was plenty of time in the morning. I wanted to sleep, but my mother kept insisting and asked me if I could come and have a look at the emails that were addressed to me. I got out of bed, and sat in the living room next to my mother at the table.

'The e-mails come from all over the world,' she said. 'Look, from New York, Scotland, and Australia.

They are from journalists. I understand very well that you are tired, but I do not know what to do with them. They are all looking for you. I have already answered as many mails as possible.'

She looked at me with a helpless look and I felt sorry for her, but my eyes fell shut.

'Sorry, but is it all right if I go back to bed for a little while? Tell them I will answer as quickly as I can.'

'Yes, of course. You go back to sleep for a few hours,' she said full of understanding.

I gave her a kiss on her forehead and walked back to my room, where I crawled into bed and immediately fell into a deep sleep.

'Wake up!'

Again, I was awakened, this time by my father. It was light outside. I walked to the bathroom to refresh myself, and in the corner of my eye, I saw that Dad was phoning and my mother was sitting at the computers. In itself, this was nothing special, but it was very early for it. As soon as my father had finished a conversation, the telephone rang again. The phone had been ringing since 5 o'clock. The emails kept coming in uninterrupted. There were messages from talk shows, but also journalists from newspapers and radio stations wanted to know the whole story behind the cheetah clip. It was a big mystery to me how they found our phone numbers and email addresses. They wanted permission to broadcast the video, which was required, but apparently, this rule did not apply to the late news of the previous evening. Up to now, my father had been able to stall for time, by saying that I was still asleep. He suggested they would call back at a later time. International news channels had heard of the incident and requested interviews. I looked at Facebook, Twitter, and YouTube. I saw that my images were shared everywhere; this is customary on social media, but for the mainstream media it's different. Then it is a matter of rights to broadcast a video. That morning, my father had been approached several times by companies who wanted to buy the license. Until then, he had managed to put them off. I did not want to sell the rights, but I got the feeling that I would not be able to keep this under control for long.

Meanwhile, there were journalists at our garden gate, hoping for an interview on camera. They had lifted the rods for sound recordings in the air. It's a good thing my father had closed the gate the night before. They were rather pushy and wanted to make an interview with the three of us. I agreed, and eventually my mother did as well. My father, on the other hand, did not feel like it and declined the request.

While my mother and I were talking to film crews outside, my father was controlling everything indoors as well as he could. He now had a notepad full of notes. When the people of the press had left, he let the phone ring for a minute to tell us that one company had made an offer to manage the license for us, which was a variation.

'I know that this is not what you want, but to stop us from worrying, I think it is a good idea to take their offer. Then I don't have to pay attention to all those requests anymore and we can focus on the journalists. I propose that we take their offer. Otherwise, there is a danger that they just broadcast it anyway and then we have to chase them for the rights. That seems impossible to me.'

He had spoken with conviction, but I reluctantly signed the contract that my father had printed out. He gave me a list with phone numbers of journalists who wanted a phone interview. I called the first number of the list and I was slightly nervous. A friendly man on the other side of the line took the call. He asked me his questions that I answered with hesitation. After the third conversation, I was not nervous anymore and I could give my answers smoothly.

My father asked me if I wanted to go on TV.

'Yes, all right,' I replied, as if this was business as usual for me. My father arranged a press conference at a local beach pavilion. He did not want any more mess in the house than there already was from the boxes for our removal.

After I finished the last phone call, and relaxed for a moment, my father told me that I would be expected to give television interviews in about an hour.

'I'll join you,' my mother said as she gave me a fresh cup of tea. For the first time that day, there was a moment of rest, and in silence, we drank our tea and coffee. We were overwhelmed by it all.

My father had chosen a summer location, a pavilion by the sea, not far from our house. The owner thought that the recordings being made was not a problem and the press conference would start at 1500 hours. It was a sunny day.

In order to get to the beach pavilion, we had to trudge through the loose sand a few hundred meters, something my father had not thought of and that was not appreciated by the film crews. Nor by my mother, but when everyone finally arrived at the pavilion, the interviews started. By now, I had my story ready thanks to the conversations I had earlier in the day. As a result, I was not surprised by the questions they asked me with the difference that I had to pay attention to my body language and posture. When it was over, my mother and I came home to an oasis of serenity. My father was on the couch and wanted to know what it had been like.

'It went well,' I replied, 'but why is it so quiet here all of a sudden?'

'Easy,' Dad replied, 'I just pulled the plug out of the phone. Tomorrow is another day.'

That evening, I watched with astonishment as my film and the interviews I had given were shown in various tv-programs. Only a tiny part was shown of all the things my mother and I had said.

122

Soon the opinions about the video were divided into two camps. One camp found it incomprehensible that the French family, furthermore with a small child, was planning to picnic between dangerous predators, while all over the wildlife park there were large signs with warnings in various languages to keep windows and doors closed, and even to lock the doors. The other camp felt that we had not done enough to warn these people. Hundreds of times the events took place in my mind, knowing that many people had a strong opinion about it, but no one could say with certainty what he or she would have done in such a bizarre situation. In any case, it could have ended badly with disastrous consequences for the French family, and no one knows what would have happened if I had sounded my horn or had stuck my head out of the window and raised my voice. I think that by acting as I had done, I prevented worse and made the right decisions. I cannot find words to express the craziness that I would be to blame while I did not put the French family in danger. Yet, it kept lingering in my mind, and I looked at the images countless times. Why did they not react to our hand gestures, and nothing happened from the car that stood next to them? Why did they ignore the signs? Why did the family get out of the car twice? That they had no idea that they put themselves at risk and this was inconceivable, because really, nobody could be that stupid. The dark-haired woman was well aware that it was dangerous, because she kept an eye on the cheetahs at all time and the child was never more than an arm length away from her. With my head full of questions that I had no answer to, I went to bed, where I could not get to sleep despite the exhausting day. I stayed awake all night.

The question *why* kept running through my head.

Chapter 22

An e-mail came in on my mobile phone asking me to
verify that I had changed my password on my FB page. I
did not accept the request because I had not changed
anything. It looked like someone was trying to hack me.
A few hours later, we received a phone call from the
company that managed the rights of our film. It turned
out that a version of the video had appeared on Facebook
and someone claimed that I had given permission for
that. I was not aware of any wrongdoing and I am hardly
active on Facebook anyway. I logged in to see what was
going on. My page had me as the main user and two
moderators: Lucas and my mother. This had been set up a
while ago for Lucas and had never been updated, while it
should have been. There was only one message in the
inbox, and the messages my mother and I had sent in the
past were nowhere to be seen. I scrolled through the
recently sent messages and came across this text: 'So you
are the maker of this video, what is your name?' and the
reply was, 'It's okay to use this video, but what kind of
contract are we talking about?' My name was at the
bottom of the message. I also found other messages of
the same nature. Lucas must have stolen my identity.
Then he was the one who had tried to delete my
password! I wanted to know immediately if this was the
case so I phoned him. While trying to stay as calm as
possible, I asked him if he had been the person who had
answered questions on my Facebook page.

'No, I don't know what you are talking about,' Lucas replied. I confronted him with the e-mails I had on my screen and after a long discussion, he finally admitted that he had indeed given answers in my name.

'Lucas, why did you do that, you prick!' I shouted at him. His answer was as disconcerting as it was incomprehensible.

'I only did it to help you and to save you from all these hectics,' he said. He also admitted that he had deleted the e-mails from my mother and me and that he had given permission to some parties to use the cheetah film. However, when he received the contracts by e-mail in order to confirm his commitments, he had become apprehensive. To cover it up, he had removed messages, but in order to delete all messages, he needed my login because I was the main user.

'You committed identity fraud,' I said, 'and that is punishable and I will report this.'
Lucas was shocked and begged for forgiveness on the pretext that he only had good intentions.

'I really did not sign anything,' he said.

When we found out about this, we could inform the license company about all the details. Fortunately, they were rather unimpressed and said that this was something that happened sometimes. We did not have to worry and they were convinced that I was in good faith. They solved all problems with the angry 'contractors' who were waiting for their signed agreements. From the contact between Lucas' mother and my mother, we learned that the failure to sign was a blessing in disguise. She also said that Lucas was very upset about it and that he really regretted it. He had been involved in a collision a few weeks ago and he had signed something that proved that the accident was his fault, even though it really wasn't. His mother had made him to understand that he should never again negligently sign an agreement. Apparently, this was something he had remembered and so the ultimate damage for us remained limited. My mother felt sorry for Lucas when she heard from his mother that I was his only friend. She adjusted her opinion and I forgave him. I had enough other concerns on my mind.

About a week after the incident, I received a message from an old friend of mine.

'Did you know about this?' he wrote. 'They want to sue you.'

My reaction to his message was matter-of-fact, but I did look for the information. A pedantic professor of media sciences thought that my parents and I should be taken to court. To my horror, I was publicly accused of shaming in the newspaper, while the professor was now doing exactly that towards me. Where did this man get the idea to sue me? The word 'maybe' was used a lot in the article that ended with 'but anyway'. Behind closed doors, I fulminated against the professor. In fact, I may have saved those people, instead of deserving punishment for my actions! He had undoubtedly received praise once for his publications, but this article was of the same questionable quality as the pseudo-scientific investigations of charlatan, Diederik Stapel, who had been sentenced to community service for his work. I had never heard of this professor and he had not contacted me, and neither had the journalist of the article. It made me furious, but when I had calmed down, I laughed about it and considered it an unachievable attempt. I did not think he had a case and took it lightly. It affected my mother in the depth of her heart.

'He does not stand a chance,' I said, but she was completely defeated and took it personally. She cried uncontrollably. If there is one thing my mother cannot stand, it is injustice, and now this was done to her son and her family. She was severely weakened by her high blood pressure and by the events of the past week. Now this on top of it. I feared that the stress would become too much for her.

The following day I received a phone call from a journalist during my lunch break.

'Have you read the article about the professor?' he asked.

'I do not want to respond to that,' I said gruffly.
He tried to convince me that it would be a good idea to say something about it, but I did not want to give a

pedestal to the nutty professor. A yes/no game would only be profitable for him and the journalist of the newspaper. I had nothing to gain from it. The professor appeared in an interview on the internet radio during which he showed his true nature for the second time. The video had been edited. The sound fragment of the first time the French family got out of the car had been attached to the second video, which made it sound like we did not take it seriously and reacted facetiously. It made me furious once again. Thankfully, a lawyer in the studio understood what was going on.

'The images do not match with the sound fragments,' he said without hesitation.

The professor muttered a bit, but the presenter came up with an argument for which the professor had no reply. Although the presenter should have checked the video-audio material in advance, I am grateful that he rectified it in the end. That lawyer is a hero.

The whole story still had a consequence, because the Public Prosecutor had to make a decision, but - as was expected from people with common sense - they announced a week later that we had not done anything unlawful. They realized that the French family was to blame for their actions and not the person who had filmed it. Finally, my mother could breathe a sigh of relief and we could close this chapter. I focused on the normal things in life again.

After a tiring week, I came home from work. I was happy the weekend had finally arrived. The work shifts played havoc with my sleep rhythm.

'Your video has been watched more than five million times,' my father said at the breakfast table on Saturday. I saw that he had checked this on his phone and that was the first time I realized that there were so incredibly many. Normally, I would have been overjoyed, but now I could not be pleased about it. Sighing, I added the last vlogs of my trip to Japan to my YouTube channel. So it would be clear for visitors once more that I was not just the maker of the cheetah video. My thoughts went back to my trip to Japan and I thought back to our group guide. I had his WhatsApp-data and I decided to send him a message. We had not had any contact for a few weeks, although I loved to keep in touch with him.

'Hey, do you remember our conversation about my YouTube channel when we were in Osaka? I think you might become famous after all,' I typed.
I immediately got a response.

'Really? That would be fun, ' he wrote.
We switched to the video function of WhatsApp so we could also see each other. We talked and laughed about the beautiful and special days in Japan. I told him about the video I had made in the wildlife park. He almost fell over from amazement.

'This video was all over the news here in Japan,' he said. I did not expect this and he had not realized it came from me. He was happy for me that my channel had so much attention and at the end of our conversation he wished me the very best. He was in a hurry because he had a group waiting for him.

That afternoon, I saw something on the internet: 'Writer ventures to remarkable theory', headlined the Brabants Dagblad online and I read it with full attention. The writer Han Peeters stated that for him it was no more than a publicity stunt of the wildlife park. 'Very clever, no advertising campaign can match this,' he added. His statement was that the French family had been hired to act the part. He had no proof of this, but by combining the improbabilities, he had reached his remarkable conclusion. There was a summary of what he thought was strange about it, and he concluded that they got out of the car twice to make sure that they had caught the filmer's attention, who had of course been thrown into a fright.

'Now there is even a conspiracy theory about the video!' I yelled to my parents.

'For real?' my mother said in amazement and at the same time, she was indignant: 'Well, I can assure them that it's real, what we've been through,' she said.

'It's not like that,' I said, 'just read.'
That night the telephone rang and I picked it up. It turned out to be another journalist.

'Did you read that article in the newspaper about that writer, Han Peeters, in which he states that it is a conspiracy?' he asked. 'Do you want to comment on that?'

'Yes, I read that piece and no, I do not comment on it, because I do not think it is useful. Everyone is entitled to his opinion, and I think enough is enough and I do not want to add fuel to the fire.'

After the verbal death threats, I had more than enough of it and from the reactions to the newspaper article, I knew that the statements were not something for which the writer was thanked. He was utterly insulted in the reactions to the article. After a host of celebrities, biologists, politicians, scientists, endless negative comments and an unreliable friend, I was more than fed up. The video was even discussed in the Lower House! I was recognized on the street and even people who knew me before did not talk about anything else. I did not know where all this would lead to. It frightened me, especially the threats. But, 'Barking dogs do not bite,' I told myself after a while and with that thought in mind I had got over it. I did not want to stir it up again. Many comments concerned my laughter in the video, but people who know me know that this is what I am like, I am always laughing. Even in my written messages I use 'ha-ha' all the time. The result was that I became very suspicious, especially after what Lucas had done to me. I had forgiven him, but I might have done that too soon. In the last conversation I had with him, I said that I simply did not have the energy anymore to get angry. Too much had happened and my emotional life had suffered some heavy blows. That is why I had forgiven him, but actually, I was not ready.

The weeks flew by and my colleagues were surprisingly mild about the video. They actually thought it was funny. I was often greeted at work with 'Hey superstar!' It sounded through all halls. A colleague had put my video on Facebook on his timeline and added a respectful text. This made me feel good. In my village in Zeeland, everyone talked to me about the video. They saw me as the local national hero, but I did not need that at all. I did not want to be a hero or superstar, but I was happy that everyone in my immediate environment acted in a normal way.

Joris and Henk did not give their opinion, from which, I concluded that they were in the camp of people who felt that I had acted wrong. They kept their mouth shut about it and that was it.

Chapter 23

I had planned my holiday for the end of May and I was
looking forward to it, because the atmosphere had
gradually changed. I was treated in a detached way and I
felt that there was gossip about me behind my back. I got
the impression that they wanted to get rid of me,
especially since Joris suddenly found that my attitude
was slack, which was totally unjustified, but he hinted
that I had to change quickly if I wanted to keep working
in the company.

The last working day before my holiday, Henk was once
again extremely annoying and on the evening of my first
holiday, I received a call from the personnel department.
I immediately knew what was up. They informed me that
I had been fired on June 1, and the only reason they gave
was that I had not been eager enough.

'But what about Henk?' I asked in vain, but I did not get
an answer to my question.

In addition to at least five official complaints against
Henk - none of these was from me - he had also
provoked the irritation of an important customer of the
company, who absolutely did not want to deal with him
anymore. There was no mention of the video, but I was
sure it had something to do with it. In my application
procedure, I was screened intensively, as they did with
every possible newcomer. Being 'vulnerable to blackmail'
was seen as a serious reason to reject someone. An
outstanding parking fine was enough for an exit, so to

speak. Everything was investigated in that research and few came through the screening. I had passed through with flying colors, but apparently, I had become a business risk because of the video. I had successfully completed the courses that I had followed in the six months I worked there, so that could not be the reason. In spite of everything, I enjoyed my work, I took on the rotten jobs and my father did not spare me on the days that I was working with him. On the contrary, just to show that I was absolutely not favored.

Bad behavior was left untouched by the company and hard-working colleagues were fired.

How stupid is that!

I just did not get it. I was not allowed to say goodbye to the colleagues with whom I had worked pleasantly, I was thrown out of the WhatsApp group of the company and not allowed to show myself on the work floor. All this at the beginning of my vacation that was not a vacation, because the move would swallow up all my time. While we had just moved to West Brabant in order to live closer to the company!

I had a two-year contract with a notice period of one month. Therefore, dismissal on 1st of June was impossible. We requested the assistance of a lawyer who looked glum at my announcement that I had been employed for only six months.

'I expect that I can get at most one month's salary for you,' he said, and he was surprised when they made a settlement of a few months.

All in all, the video had completely turned my life upside down. I hated it and I wished it never happened. Now, I wanted to be left alone!

Chapter 24

Fast, but not too fast, Nikita drove over the wildlife park towards the exit. In her mirror, she saw that Malev was driving closely behind her.

'It was actually more exciting than I had thought beforehand,' Milena said. 'If it had been lions or tigers, we would not have survived.'

Heinrich put his photo camera away and Milena asked him if he had taken pictures, but he said he had not.

'The thing has been broken for years,' he said.

A little further up there was a congestion of cars with visitors who wanted to have a good look at some animal or other. Nikita and Malev steered along and the road ahead was free.

'I hope we can get out of here,' Milena said.

She was worried about the park rangers who had driven past just after they had got out the second time, but they were nowhere to be seen. If someone had raised the alarm, the exit was undoubtedly blocked. She called Malev.

'What do we do if the exit is blocked?' she asked.

His answer did not surprise her. According to Malev, they had to drive on at full throttle regardless of possible damage.

'Okay,' she said, and she conveyed the message to Nikita who gripped the steering wheel so tight again that her knuckles were white.

Meanwhile in Malev's car, Vladimir restored the back seat, where he had been lying under a blanket with his stun gun at the ready. His view of the group had been limited, but if the cheetahs had attacked them, he would certainly have hit two. Fortunately, this had not happened and he did not have to recharge his gun for a third shot. He had been surprised that three cheetahs were involved, but he kept extra cartridges within reach just in case anyway. Recharging would take time and he had told Malev so, but Malev remained stoic about it.

'If they do it well, shooting will not be necessary. If it is, then it will be their own stupid fault,' he had said. Because most of their joint luggage was in Malev's car, it took some effort to get the back seat in the right position again, but he managed after a few minutes. He also placed the rifle back under his seat and he crawled in the passenger's seat.

'So far, the Lord has been on our side,' he said, and he wiped sweat drops from his forehead with his sleeve. They drove past the congestion and now that the road was clear he gestured to Nikita that she had to drive faster, which was a risk, because there were animals along the way.

'There is the exit,' Nikita said after a while, and to her great relief it had not been blocked. 'We're damn lucky with this,' she said while she drove onto the public road outside the park. Milena and Heinrich also breathed a sigh of relief.

'Do you have the address of that second hotel in Reims?' she asked Heinrich.

He mentioned it and Milena typed it in the navigation device. They were still tense and expected to be forced into the curb at any moment, but nothing happened. Neither did they spot any helicopters, which would certainly be used during a manhunt. Nothing of all this. Malev phoned and Milena answered.

'As soon as we are on the highway, I will pass you and you will drive to Reims without exceeding the speed limit. Do you have the address?'

'Yes, Heinrich gave it to me.'

Malev gave her a new address in the vicinity of the hotel. This place was the one he had agreed with Hector as the pick-up point for the cars so the license plates could be changed back.

'You did a fantastic job, Milena,' he said. 'I am very proud of you. Executed to perfection and I saw that the man in the grey car filmed it all. Let's hope he puts it online.'

'Thank you,' Milena replied, 'I'll talk to you later.'

In Reims, Hector had been waiting for Malev and his crew for at least an hour. From that afternoon, he had carefully monitored all news channels, but nothing had been reported about the action. That reassured him, because that meant that the action had been successful. On the other hand, it was also possible that the action had not taken place at all for one reason or another. He had set Google Alerts to the search term 'cheetah' on his laptop and linked it to his e-mail address. He would automatically receive a message if a cheetah were in the news. He steadily looked at his inbox every few seconds, but nothing popped up. His uncertainty as to whether or not it had succeeded made him crazy. Finally, after two hours of waiting, Malev parked behind him. Malev and Vladimir got out, walked over to Hector's car, and sat down in the back seat.

'And...?' Hector asked. 'Has the action been successful?' The men recounted how the action had been performed in all its colorful details. It had been a great success, although it would actually only be successful if the video came online, something they could not influence. Hector congratulated the men and handed Malev the final envelope with 15,000 euros and separately one with 5,000 euros for the expenses incurred and as thanks for the service provided. It was eagerly accepted by Malev.

'When will the rest of your crew arrive?' Hector asked Malev called Nikita and it turned out they were only a few miles from the destination. Malev passed that on to Hector and he ended the conversation.

'Load your stuff in this car and then you can drive to the hotel,' Hector said. 'You unload everything there and check in, and once that's done, you can pick up the others here. Tomorrow night I will place the two cars back here when they have been restored to their original state, but I assume that you will drive to Cologne on Wednesday morning.'

Malev said that this was indeed the intention.

   'Oh yes, I almost forgot. You have to close this car at the hotel and put a possible exit ticket under the sun visor. Please place the key on top of the right rear wheel. Tomorrow night we will need this car again to get home.' Together they moved the things to the other car and Malev and Vladimir drove away in the car with which Hector had come. They had just gone out of sight when Nikita and the others appeared. Hector greeted them and saw that the women and certainly the children were very tired of the long journey. They emptied the car and put everything on the sidewalk. Hector took over the car.

   'In fifteen minutes Malev will be here to pick you up, but I expect he may even be sooner than that. Thank you for your fantastic cooperation and goodbye.'

When he drove off, he gave them an exuberant thumb up as a token of appreciation that they had done so well. With this car, he drove to the mechanic who once again had a day to put everything in order. He collected Malev's car as quickly as possible with the car mechanic. Everything had taken place exactly as Hector had planned and he was extremely satisfied with it, but according to Google Alerts it was still not in the news.

Chapter 25

Hector had his eyes focused on his inbox that night, and twice his heart skipped a beat, but it turned out to be a false alarm, and then a third message with the keyword 'cheetah' appeared on his screen. He saw that there was a video and he clicked on it. Hector recognized the tree on the wildlife park and studied what was going on around it. About a minute later, he had seen it and put his arms in the air with joy. They showed up very well in video and it looked natural. He thought it was a pity that it did not show what had happened before. Immediately, viewers had responded to it, which made him cheerful. Most of them were shocked and condemned the French family, as they were called. There was a lot of discussion about it, but the number of views did not rise quickly. Hector was looking for a method to make the video go viral, but that way he might betray himself. He decided to wait until it spread like a wildfire, no matter how impatient he was. He had to lie low until Malev and his crew were safely back in Moldova. He did not want to risk them being recognized at the hotel or at the airport in Cologne, which was not inconceivable if the item exploded on the internet. If it had not broken through on Thursday, he could think of a plan. Perhaps he could leak it to a news channel, that asked people on their website to send extraordinary videos to the editors.

As agreed, the cars with the German license plates were put in place and he walked with the car mechanic to the hotel, where they picked up the car in which they drove back. The mechanic was generously rewarded for his services.

The next afternoon Hector drove to Reims to see if the cars were still there, which was not the case. He was relieved about it. They had left and were expected to arrive in their home country the next day. They would be home Thursday afternoon at the latest, and to be on the safe side, he would wait another day to give publicity to the video one way or another. It had been changed on the YouTube channel; now the first scene was shown as well. The number of viewers was not yet spectacular; then it went loose and he did not have to do anything about it. It went viral all by itself. Lex could be satisfied and Hector looked back on a supremely successful action for everyone involved.

Chapter 26

A week after the action that had been excellent, Hector was invited to Lex's castle again. It was an unexpected invitation for the man of the hour, and Hector felt as if he had risen far above himself. All the effort he had made and all the thinking that had preceded it, would now lead to his appreciation and in the meantime, he had helped his son earn a lot of money for himself. The evaluation would be the springboard to eternal fame in the function of master within the order. That would yield even more profit for him than what he had accumulated so far. Humming, Hector drove past the steel gate of the castle and reported himself to the guard in the lodge. The gate closed behind Hector and he was allowed to proceed to the main building, where Lex was waiting for him. With his tires crackling on the white gravel, his car stopped and Lex shook his hand before he had even got out of his car.

'Welcome, Master Almagnac - le Noir,' Lex said and he gave his guest a wink. Hector thanked him for the praise.

'Come in, and tell me everything about your brilliant action,' Lex said, and he introduced Hector to his office on the first floor. The room was attractively furnished with lots of woodwork and a whole wall full of leather-bound books that turned their backs on them. Now Hector understood why he had been invited to the hunting room the last time and that it had been Lex' intention to explain to him about the triceratops, to put

Hector on a track that resulted in the intended result. The grandmaster may have called him 'brilliant', but Lex should not forget his own role in this.

After the coffee ritual, identical to that of his previous visit, Lex asked him about the details and Hector told him the whole story in chronological order, and he saw that Lex was thoroughly enjoying himself. He praised Hector regularly for his thinking and the decisions he had made.

'What I did not expect is that the recording has had such a huge impact and has already been viewed six million times,' Hector said. 'The man who made it and his parents have been flooded with media attention from all over the world and almost all news channels and talk shows have paid attention to it.'

He said it to confirm the success for himself.

'Yes, and you could not have been more successful in that. The number of visitors has risen like a rocket, ' Lex said, 'but we have to hold their attention, so I approached an old friend of mine, who is a professor, to add extra enthusiasm to the discussion. I asked his opinion about the incident, and just that was a signal for him to come up with something.'

'Okay, I'm curious, ' Hector said, and for a moment, he thought very deeply about whether to say it, but decided to do it anyway.

'There is only one person who has realized that it is an act. He has congratulated the wildlife park on their

Facebook page with their promotional stunt. A journalist from a regional newspaper noticed the message and published the story, after which it was reproduced by a few other local papers. They did not believe that it was a promotion stunt, but it adds extra attention for the park. So he is right, but maybe we can do something with it.'
Lex looked at him with raised eyebrows. Apparently, he had not been aware of it and Hector began to doubt whether he had done well to report it.

'That has escaped my attention,' Lex said. 'Is it online too?'

'Yes,' Hector said, and he told his host where he could find it. Lex fetched his tablet and entered the search data. Immediately his face turned white and his sharp jaw line became visible. He read it and cursed.

'Do you know who this is?' Lex asked in a grim tone. Hector shrugged and said he did not know him.

'This is Han Peeters, a writer, and he has already written two books in which I, Moneytron and Chateau des Amerois appear. I do not know his sources, but I suspect he spoke with a former brother. The detailed information that he divulges in his books is of such a nature that we cannot reach a different conclusion. I have already received worried questions from the top of the Ministry of Justice and Security and from a judge who is described in a covert manner in one of the books of that bastard. The judge recognized himself in the description. If Peeters decides to write a book about this story as well, there will be an uproar. It could even lead to the end of the royal houses in Belgium, the Netherlands, in England, and the fall of the parliamentary democracies in this part of Europe. Peeters is dangerous for us. He has a strong growing number of followers and readers. His books are also available physically and as e-books in the Netherlands and Belgium from all booksellers, including bookshops that exclusively sell online. Three of his books have been translated into English and can be ordered worldwide. Do not underestimate this man.'

'It surely will not have that kind of impact,' Hector said somewhat frightened.

'We seriously take into account that the influence of this writer can be enormous. He not only mentions the abuse that, according to him, goes on in the circles of the 'uber-elite', as he calls them, but he has also rewritten the constitution, which is also published in book form. In this book, he states in non-fiction that it is high time feudalism is abolished, and that it must be replaced with a new system in which there will no longer be any need for those who still enjoy immunity now. Imagine what that means to us and that is only part of his idiotic vision. He also tackles the monetary system and establishes a self-cleaning democracy with binding referenda without political leaders.'

'But that's impossible,' Hector said.

'Listen,' Lex said, and sat at the edge of his chair. He leaned forward.

'We have been in control for the past five thousand years. We do not care who is in power in the world, because we are the real rulers. What we want will be accomplished. Think for example of abolishing the dividend tax. That is not thought up by the Prime Minister himself. We have told him to do it, and he adheres to it. It is usually a mutual agreement, but not all political leaders know that they are being used. Did you really think that a passenger plane was shot by a base unit of an army under the command of a world leader? Oh no, that happened upon instructions from us by our own people and no one else knows anything about this. Meanwhile, we can drill for shale gas in that area without difficulties. We set populations up against each other and harvest in, for example, arms deliveries. The people like being fooled and they believe what they see. Look at your own example of the wildlife park. It is too simple for words if you compare it with the world stage, but it does have a big influence. Prior to the internet, the world was well arranged for us. The internet has changed that, but now that we know how to deal with it, we are on track to reach our sacred goal.'

'And what would that be?' Hector asked.

'You can do a search for it later when you're home,' Lex replied, 'you can find it under the term: Georgia Guide stones. But more about Han Peeters. He writes in his books about Freemasonry and the Illuminati in every possible way. Also about our Satanism, and the - in his eyes - disgusting habits with regard to paedo-sexual rituals. With his books, he can unleash a great popular anger against us. Realize that we still have a strong grip on everything, but numerically we are far in the minority. That is a big problem for us and we are not afraid of anything except for a domination by the people, which of course will cause chaos, something Peeters also refers to. In case of chaos, his plans are ready for the establishment of a new democracy, in which the people really come to power and all world problems for the mob are resolved. If he writes a book about your action and it becomes a success, he will reach many new readers with his backward ideology, which he will undoubtedly incorporate into his story again.'

'Are you really afraid that a popular anger can develop?' Hector asked.

His voice had a sound of incredulity.

'Yes, of course, why do you think we have broken down the Round House in Nunspeet to the last stone and there are many castles in Belgium, also called haunted castles, that have been left to their fate and have been largely destroyed. The trees grow out of the roofs, but the buildings and the domains are not sold under any circumstances. The human remains that can still be found there would be the deathblow for everything we stand for. Nothing, absolutely nothing, must stand in our way.'

'But if that Han Peeters is such a big danger, then he will just be dealt with,' Hector thought.

'That's a misconception,' Lex replied. 'If we do that, then we will put the emphasis on him and his books. In any case, we will help him with a lot of publicity. The information he has given in his books means that there will be an in-depth research of our activities and then it will be over and done for us in no time. The man lives on an estate and hardly shows himself in public. He is not militant and does not stand on the barricades, but we do know that he is preparing a new world order - with extremely disastrous consequences for us. If we deal with him, we emphasize his claims. Then it comes back as a boomerang and we confirm his vision. We do not do anything physically to him and we wait, but we will try to discredit him. The problem is that he writes in faction, which means fiction based on facts. Because of his form of writing, he is inviolable in Western democracies and he does not use the names of the real people in his books, but his readers know who he writes about, or can easily find it on the internet.'

Now Hector knew for certain that he should not have mentioned it.

'Let's hope it blows over,' he said.

Lex agreed and although the conversation was different from what Hector had imagined, they returned to the subject of his action and that he would be rewarded with the title of master in the order.

Chapter 27

On the last day of the crowdfunding of the project, the counter stopped at 5.8 million euros, which provided for Hector a nice additional 40,000 euros. The money plus interest had to be repaid by his son to the investors, but that did not matter to Hector. After all, it was a piece of cake for Daan. Hector knew it would not be a problem and his son had already transferred the provision of 235,000 euros to him. Hector had taken a big step forward and as a Bokito, he beat himself on the chest. Now he felt that it was high time that he joined a dating website to find a partner he would like to spend his money on. He soon realized that there was plenty of choice and on the first day, his profile was already visited by dozens of women. He selected among the women who had sent him at least one heart, and his goal was to lure one between 35 and 40 years old. Children were serious obstacles and welfare mothers were out of the question for him anyway. They had a chance if they looked nice and had a bit of class. Hector had posted a passport photo of himself of some fifteen years ago, which he thought was the standard in the merry-go-round of the dating industry. According to him, it was nothing more than a big meat market, but he was longing for some company, and sex, and if she did not make too many dumb statements, he would be up for it. It astonished him that it took so much time to find a suitable date who could be a good match for him, until he shifted his focus slightly to women between the ages of 40 and 45. Many of them had children, but they no longer lived at home and in terms of looks, it almost made no difference. He spoke to a 43-year-old woman, a former English teacher, who also did not live too far away from him, which was another selection criterion. After exchanging a lot of messages and cautious attempts to discuss sex, he had a date with her and agreed to meet in a restaurant. Her name was Stephanie and that did not match her sultry nickname on the dating platform. She had more weight in real life than on her profile, but that also applied to him, and after they both felt found out and had to laugh about themselves, the ice was broken. They got on very well. It helped that Hector knew a lot about English literature with which he kept the conversation going. As the evening progressed, he began to find her more and more attractive, and he hoped that these feelings were mutual.

'I really enjoyed meeting you,' he said after paying the bill. He waited anxiously for her reply.

'I also enjoyed the dinner and your company,' she said, which Hector regarded as a stronger statement than the one he had made. Sex was out of the question for him on this night, and anyway, the longer you wait for something, the better it is when you finally get it. Stephanie appreciated that in him and they spoke openly and clearly about it.

'Shall we meet again?' Hector asked.

'Yes, what do you have in mind?'

Hector could have shouted that sex was in his mind mostly, but he restrained himself.

'How about we go to the wildlife park for a day,' Hector said. He said it without thinking it over, but thought it would be all right. He had always remained out of the picture, and for a moment, he felt like a murderer who always returned to the crime scene or at least went to the victim's funeral ceremony.

'You mean that park where a French family recently stepped out of the car and barely escaped death?' she asked.

Hector laughed hard and said that it was indeed that wildlife park.

'Sounds like fun,' he said.

'I think so too,' she replied

On a sunny Saturday, they drove to the wildlife park, for the occasion, Stephanie was dressed in a short skirt with tiger print, and Hector enjoyed this tremendously. It appeared the woman also had a good sense of humor.

'But you have to promise me that you will stay in the car,' he said with a smile.

A long line of cars was waiting on the emergency lane before the exit to the wildlife park. Hector knew that there were traffic lights at the end of the exit and that it would take a long time before they could enter the park. The procession had caused traffic jams even on the motorway. Hector heard this in the car via the radio and saw them on the roadways next to them.

'Is it always this busy here?' Stephanie asked.

'No,' Hector replied. 'This is the result of the huge publicity caused by that recording of the cheetahs.' Forty-five minutes later, they could finally enter the park, where they again had to drive very slowly in a long line of cars that made a tour throughout the park. Lex had told him that the visitor numbers had shot up like a rocket, but this even exceeded Hector's expectations. They enjoyed watching the animals from the car and then stretched their legs in the part of the park where this was allowed. They drank ice-tea and visited the souvenir shop. Hector stood in amazement in front of a huge shelf with plush cheetahs. Someone tapped on his shoulder and he turned around.

'Mr. Almagnac, how nice to see you here again,' a woman said, and from her uniform, he gathered she was a staff member of the park.

Hector blushed and looked at her questioningly.

'We met about ten years ago, when...you know, that campaign in Antwerp.'

'Ah,' Hector said, and now he recognized the woman.

'That was not such a clever action at the time, but in the end it worked out all right,' she said, spreading out her arms.

'You've recognized me, ' Hector said surprised.

'Well, we all have the memory of an elephant here,' she said and had to laugh at it.

'This is indeed something else,' Hector said, and he too made a wide arm gesture. 'At least the last promotion stunt has been very successful.'
Immediately Hector knew he had said too much, he apologized and walked away from her. The employee stood transfixed in utter amazement.

FIN

EPILOGUE

I hope that you enjoyed reading this book, although the reason for it was far from pleasant for the filmmaker and his parents. They were frightened wildly. Imagine what you would had done in such a bizarre situation. From his second nature, he captured the incident on film. He was blamed for this by a professor, although in this day and age, it is common practice to film what you see. Everyone makes videos of everything. In cases like this, the police will even advise people to get images that can be analyzed later on. News channels and talk shows also request on their websites that the public send in the remarkable videos they made.

Thank heavens it has ended well for the 'French family' and I am convinced that the filmmaker has done the only right thing, which has prevented it from getting worse. If they had been wounded or killed by the cheetahs, he would not have made the film public, but would have handed it over to the law.

It is his personal right that he has put this video on his YouTube channel to share what he is doing and what he experiences in his life.

The incident itself balances on the dividing line between fact and fiction. Nobody will ever just decide to take a walk among dangerous predators. The woman with the child knew it was dangerous. It is clearly visible that she was well aware of it. She did not even hesitate to take a risk twice.

'The stupid French family' dominated the media and everyone accepted it as the truth, just like that. The woman with the child on her arm was not stupid. She was an animal handler. This is my personal interpretation of the incident. I do not have to defend myself, because I am entitled to my own thoughts and am allowed to publish them. In the Netherlands, we have freedom of speech and I have made use of that, while we still can.

With the knowledge from this book, I ask you to take a look at the video again and come to your own conclusions.

The professor of media sciences can include this book as teaching material in the context of article 7 of the Dutch constitution.

HAN PEETERS

Bibliography Han Peeters (English books)

The Last Prophet (2014)
Book: 9789462170858 | E-Book: 9789462170872

The New Constitution (2016)
Book: 9789462170988 | E-book: 9789462170964

Planet X (2018)
Book: 9789462171015 | E-book: 9789462170995 |

www.hanpeeters.com